FORWARD
MARCH

CAREY ANNE FARRELL

To all past, present, and future FHS Marching Cadets.

ATTENTION

Dani's late, as usual. But I've saved her a seat. As usual.

"You know, you're ruining my life, Meghan," she says, sliding into the chair next to me. "If anyone saw me here, I'd be dead."

That's Dani's thing right now, that there's this Anyone keeping tabs on her and ranking her coolness based on everything she does. I'm pretty sure if there was Someone keeping track of people's coolness, They wouldn't even bother paying attention to us band nerds. But Dani doesn't want to be a band nerd anymore.

It took me all week to convince her to come: "It's just an informational meeting. We'll see the band. They'll tell us to join in the fall. We'll say, 'We'll think about it,' and then we'll leave."

On Monday, she said, "Uh-uh, no way in hell. As soon as freshman year's over, I'm throwing my clarinet in the dumpster."

On Tuesday, she said, "I'm chucking my clarinet, and if

1

you don't shut up about this stupid meeting, I'm taking your trombone with it." But on Wednesday, she said, "This meeting thing. It's only an hour, right?" I thought my awesome powers of persuasion had worn her down. It turned out her parents had found her clarinet in the kitchen trash can.

But it doesn't matter how we ended up here tonight. It matters that we're here, together, in the Dulaney High cafeteria, and the DHS marching band is on its way inside.

The Marching Patriots are a legend. They're one of the oldest high school bands in Maryland. They've won championships, marched in parades, traveled all over the country. And they're upperclassmen-only. But freshman year is almost over, and in a few months, I'll be out of our pathetic freshman band and into the marching band. The real thing. Where I belong.

Ms. Lozaro, the freshmen band director, introduces the drum majors, and the band boosters, and finally Mr. Coffman, the *real* band director. He's just starting at DHS, after the last guy retired, and even in the freshmen wing, we've heard the rumors about how good he is. Then the head drum major gives three quick whistle blasts, and the band explodes through the cafeteria doors in a burst of brass and drums and shiny blue and gold uniforms.

Sure, they can't really march around the cafeteria tables, but they still look great, and they're so loud my ears are ringing. They play the school fight song, and a song I remember from a car ad a few summers ago, and I'm so mesmerized by the sound and the movement that I forget to worry about what Dani's thinking. But then, they launch into "Under The Sea," from The Little Mermaid, and even though Dani and I usually lie about it, The Little Mermaid is still our favorite movie ever. We grab each other's hands and shriek, and we get up with the rest of the freshman band and sing along. By the second verse, we're totally cracking up, trying to remember the choreography we made up a hundred years ago. Maybe we look like idiots, but at least we're being idiots together.

Three more blasts from the drum majors' whistles, and the band marches out the door, cheering. I find myself saying my own cheer in my head, or maybe it's more like a prayer: "I want to be a part of this. I want to be a part of this."

We're supposed to follow them back to the band room for refreshments, but I don't think I can move yet. Dani isn't budging, either.

"Oh, my God," I breathe.

"I know," Dani says. "Senior. Drummers. Are. So. Hot."

Wait, what?

"We totally need to sign up for marching band next year," I say.

"And I totally need to talk to that guy."

"What? What guy?"

"The one…playing the drum…thing…" She trails off, staring beyond the cafeteria door.

"So, we're gonna sign up, right? For marching band?"

Dani takes my hands again, stares at me intently, and says, "How's my lipstick?"

I take that as a yes.

MARK TIME

CHAPTER ONE

I spend most of June counting down to the first day of band camp. It's not like I have anything else to do. My older sister, Nina, is freaking about starting at Swarthmore at the end of the summer. My younger sister, Ellie, is at a different day camp every week, and competing in swim meets every weekend. As for me, no one's looking to hire a fifteen-year-old with no marketable skills, even just for a few months, and our trip to Gram's house in Ocean City won't happen until later in the summer, after the Senior Week kids and most of the tourists have cleared out.

A few weeks into summer break, Dani texts me about meeting up at the pool for the afternoon. First, I think she wants some BFF bonding time. Then I find out The Hot Drummer with the Drum Thing is lifeguarding.

At the pool, Dani and I are laying out on our towels (well, she's laying out—I'm covered up in shorts, a T-shirt, and a thick coat of sunblock), and Dani's telling me how, this time next year, she's gonna be here at the pool with the Hot Drummer, and she's gonna be his girlfriend. Or she'll be some other hot drummer's girlfriend. She'll definitely be someone's girlfriend, that's for sure.

While Dani talks, I watch the other people at the pool. A couple of old guys in Speedos have taken over the lap lanes, like usual, and a bunch of kids are fighting over the inner tubes, the way Dani and I used to do. Then there's a girl a few towels away who seems familiar, and she keeps looking at us—well, at Dani—like we look familiar, too. Finally, she comes over.

"Hey," the girl says to Dani. Even though she's at the swimming pool, she's wearing more makeup on her face than I've ever bought in my life. I'm guessing she's not the kind of person who goes to the pool to swim. "Hey, you're a clarinet, aren't you?"

Dani gets this guarded look on her face, folds her arms across her bikini top, and goes, "Why?"

"No, it's cool," the girl says. "I thought I recognized you. I'm Maya. I'm the section leader this year."

"I'm Dani," Dani says, and she stands up. They're both the same height (short), complexion (tan), and build (bikini-worthy, though I know Dani still wears a padded top). Maya starts going on about some clarinet party she wants to have next week, and how Dani and all the other newbies totally have to come because it'll be so much fun, and they'll all braid each other's hair and trade reeds with each other, or whatever it is you do at an all-clarinet party, not that I'd know.

Then I hear Dani ask, in what she probably thinks is a whisper, "So...you know that lifeguard over there, right? The drummer?"

"Who, Bryce?" Maya says. "Yeah, you wanna meet him?"

Dani's so excited, she practically licks her. "Back in a minute, okay, Meghan?" she says, and she bounds away in Maya's shadow.

Not that I'm watching the pool clock or anything, but Dani's one minute? Turns into twenty.

It's weird seeing Dani flirt with a guy. I guess that's what she and Maya are doing, anyway. What's weirder is, whatever she's doing, looks like it's working. Bryce is laughing, but not in the way guys usually laugh at us. It's more like he's laughing with her. He leans down from the stand to hand her his water bottle, and even from where I'm sitting, I can tell he's checking out her padded boobs. I stare down at the sunblock streaking my legs, my arms, my ratty old gym shorts, and my giant M.R. DUCKS T-shirt from last summer's Ocean City trip. I'm used to being invisible. But I'm used to Dani being invisible with me.

The night Dani goes to the clarinet party, I get roped into helping at Ellie's swim meet, and in between scribbling out blue ribbons for little kids who can already swim faster than I ever could, I check my phone. I'm not sure whether I'm hoping for or against updates from Dani. She sends me a selfie with her and Maya and some other girls, all making the same dumb duck face. She writes, "Sorry ur not here!!!!" but it feels a lot more like, "Sorry ur not here????" But then she texts me that Maya is BFFs with the girl who might be leading the trombone section this year, and I get this stupid feeling of hope in my chest.

When I'm back home, I pick out my outfit for the first day of band camp and hang it up on my desk chair like a promise. Like it's saying, "Everything's gonna change once we get to band camp. And it's gonna be amazing."

CHAPTER TWO

The night before band camp starts, I go to bed feeling ready for anything.

Then I walk into the DHS band room the next morning, and realize I'm ready for nothing. Nothing at all.

First, I guess I kind of thought Dani would be here already, and we could face band camp together. Instead, I'm…alone.

Well, not alone. The band room is enormous—it's four rooms, really, with Mr. Coffman's office, the band locker room, and the music library besides the actual classroom—and with five minutes to go before camp starts, it's full of people. I'm just not friends with any of them.

I weave through the clumps of kids. When I see other newbies I kind of know, I smile at them. A few of them kind of smile back. Most of them don't see me.

But then I see someone else who looks familiar. The dark-haired girl over there, in the back, in the black tank top. I've seen her around before—when you're a girl who stands at 5'10" barefoot, it's hard to forget another girl who's taller than you. And look, she's taking her own trombone out of her case, too. Maybe that's Maya's friend, the one Dani was telling me about. If that's where the trombones are supposed to sit, I should walk over there anyway. And when I get there, I'll say hi. Hi, my name's Meghan. I've been introducing myself since I was four. It's no big deal. Right?

"Hi," I say to her as I put my case down next to hers. "My name's Meghan."

See? No big deal. I even got my name right.

She looks up, and there's a trace of a smile on her face as she says, "Hey, how's it going?"

"I'm fine," I say. "How are you?" And I get a second— maybe even less—to congratulate myself on being outgoing, polite, and grownup, before a guy's voice from behind me answers, "Oh, hey, Kat. What's up?"

Duh. She was talking to the guy behind me. Why would she be talking to me? She has no idea who I am. She probably didn't even hear me. She probably didn't even see me.

"What are you staring at, newbie?"

Oops. I guess she sees me now. That trace of a smile? It's a glare now. The kind of glare you give to a bug that won't die. I am a newbie. I am a bug. I stare at my trombone case and wonder if I could hide inside it for the rest of the day.

She rolls her eyes and sighs, and then she notices the trombone case I'm still clutching in my right hand. "Oh, *fuck*, you're in my section. Get over to the chairs by the trophy case and try not to piss anybody else off on your way over there."

I bite my lip and think of a million witty things I could

say back to her, if I had guts or a spine or a brain or anything. And then I step on a trumpet.

"Dude, watch out!" says the guy behind me, like it's my fault he's left his trumpet on the floor. "God, the newbies get dumber every year," he says, and Kat snorts.

I check the clock. It's only 8:59 and 56 seconds. Maybe it isn't too late to change my mind.

#

So here's what band camp's all about:

1. Marching, in the 95-degree heat.

2. Playing, in the 95-degree heat.

3. Marching and playing at the same time, in the 95-degree heat.

4. Finding out marching and playing at the same time is like patting your head and rubbing your stomach at the same time…if you're patting your head with six pounds of metal, and trying to rub your stomach so you're always rubbing on the left side on beats one and two, and on the right side on beats three and four, and every time you screw up you get yelled at. In the 95-degree heat.

5. Getting yelled at by Kat. In the 95-degree heat. It

bears repeating, because this happens a lot. Especially to me.

Stuff I get yelled at for:

1. Not rolling my feet. Forgetting to lift up my right heel as soon the ball of my left foot touches the ground. Forgetting to lift up my left heel as soon as the ball of my right foot touches the ground. Rolling too slow. Then, rolling too fast. Then, rolling too slow again.

2. Being off-step. I know I'm supposed to be on my left foot on the one and the three, and on my right foot on beats two and four. But I'm so focused on rolling my feet the right way, I can't figure out how to stay on beat anymore.

3. Finally asking a question that's been bugging me for a year: why our fight song is the Notre Dame Victory March, when we're a public high school in Maryland. Apparently, because our colors are blue and gold. And, hello, IT'S TRADITION. And traditions don't need to make sense. And I'm not supposed to talk when we're standing at attention.

4. Not marking time high enough. Then, marking time too high. Then, not marking time high enough again, and Jesus Christ, newbie, how stupid are you?

Kat's not the only other trombone, but she's one of two seniors, and she's planning to be section leader, and she puts herself next to me in all of the drills, because yelling at me is her idea of fun. By the time we break for lunch, I'm ready to go home and hide under my bed for the rest of my life. But I know Nina can't pick me up until camp's over at 5, so instead of running home, I run to the clarinet section to find Dani.

She and some of the other clarinet girls have pushed their chairs into a circle. I say her name a few times, but she doesn't hear me, and when I realize how creepy I must look, lurking behind her, I finally tap her on the shoulder.

"What?" she says, sounding less than thrilled. "Can I sit with you guys?"

Dani looks around the circle, which is pretty squished already.

"I can grab that chair over there," I offer, pointing to an empty chair in the flute section.

She sighs. "Um, you guys? Can everyone scooch over a little? For Meghan?"

The other girls start moving their chairs, sighing like it's the hardest thing anyone's ever asked them to do. But the important thing is they're moving. Right?

I grab the chair from the flute section, and I'm gone a second, maybe two, but by the time I get back to the clarinets, my spot is taken. By Maya. And Kat.

They turn around and stare at me.

"Oh, were you sitting here?" Maya asks, in what could

almost pass for real concern.

Dani jumps up. "Maya, this is Meghan. Is it okay if she sits with us?"

"We met at the pool," I say helpfully.

Maya eyes me the same way Kat did when I got in her way this morning—the same way Kat's still eyeing me. Like they're this close to taking me out with a flyswatter.

"Newbie-free zone," Kat says.

"Sorry, Meghan," Maya says.

"Sorry, Meghan," echoes Dani. Dani who is also a newbie. Last I checked, anyway.

I take my lunch to the bathroom.

I'm pretty sure the day can't get any worse. But then, after lunch, the drum majors make us march backwards.

They don't bother to tell us how we're supposed to do it —one of them just yells, "BACKWARDS, MARCH!" and in that split second where I hesitate, and try to figure it out, Kat steps back right into my trombone slide.

She screams like I've stabbed her in the back with six pounds of metal. Which, okay, I have. But I didn't mean to. If she should be yelling at anybody, it's the drum majors. Not me. Kat goes home early to ice her back, and no one but Dani will talk to me for the rest of the day. Even she keeps sneaking glances at Maya and the other clarinets while we're talking, like they're gonna kick her out of the section or something for talking to me. I can't wait to get out of there.

#

"So how was your first day of band camp, Meghan?"
Mom asks, as she passes me the tomato sauce across the
dinner table. Dad's working late again tonight, which
means Mom's cooking, which means spaghetti. My parents
talk a lot about how important family dinners are, and how
we're all supposed to have conversations and bond and
stuff. I think Mom might have read about it in one of those
parenting books, back when we were babies, and it's
definitely one of those things that works way better in
parenting books than in real life. Half the time, Dad's
working late; the other half of the time, Mom's working
late; and Nina, Ellie, and I have nothing to say to each
other. Yeah, we look alike—we're all tall like Dad, and we
all have Mom's wild, curly light brown hair and blue eyes—
but that's as far as it goes. And having the same eye color
isn't enough to bond you to somebody. I mean, you know
who else has blue eyes? Kat.

Speaking of which…"I don't know if I want to talk
about it," I say. What I mean is, I don't want to talk to
Mom about it. I want to talk to Dani, but she isn't
answering my texts.

"Did they seriously make you march for eight hours
straight?" asks Nina.

I think about it for a second. "Yeah. Actually, they did."
And then the whole story comes pouring out after all.
Mom makes sympathetic noises. Nina rolls her eyes when

she's supposed to. Even Ellie listens.

When I get to the part about hitting Kat with my trombone slide, Nina cracks up. "Wait," she says. "Kat Rossi?"

"Yeah."

"Oh, my God, I hate her. She's a total bitch."

"Nina! Watch your language!"

"Sorry, Mom. But it's true. She's one of those girls with PMS 365 days a year."

"Nina! Not in front of Ellie!"

"Why not?" Ellie demands. "Hello, I'm going into fifth grade. I already saw the movie."

"What movie?"

"Mom. The *movie*. They made us all watch it in gym, and then they gave us maxi pads and the boys teased us for a whole week."

"Anyway," Nina adds, "I bet half the girls in Ellie's class already have their periods."

"God, thanks, Nina." Ellie scowls at her spaghetti.

"Really, Nina," Mom says, "can we please not talk about this at the dinner table? Meghan, you were telling us about…about…"

"Band camp, Mom." I try not to sound too annoyed. It's not her fault I'm the middle child.

"Right," says Nina. "Kat Rossi. Remember? She lived across the street from us when I was in fourth grade."

"In the Bunches' house?" Ellie asks.

"No, the house next door to theirs." She gestures with

her fork. "With that old guy who doesn't put his shirt on when he goes out to get the mail."

"Yuck," says Ellie.

"His name is Mr. Wright," Mom says, "and he's very nice. You know your grandmother went out to lunch with him, when she was here over Easter. He used to be a biology teacher."

"Ew, Mr. Wright," Ellie giggles. "More like Mr. Wrong."

"Band camp," I say, a little louder this time.

"You don't remember when Kat lived across the street from us? Maybe you repressed it," says Nina. "She spent that whole summer teasing you because you couldn't do a cartwheel."

"That sounds like her," I say. "She's awful."

"365 days of the year," Nina says again.

"Can't you talk to your section leader about this?" Mom asks.

That's it, I'm done. I clear my place and head for the sink. "It probably wouldn't help," I call over my shoulder, "considering Kat might be my section leader."

"Hey, at least you know how to do a cartwheel now," Nina offers.

"Great," I say. "I'll show her tomorrow. I bet we'll be best friends before we even start learning the show."

CHAPTER THREE

Here's what actually happens. First thing Tuesday morning, Colleen, the head drum major, herds all the trombones into the music library, saying we've gotta talk about Something Important. Kat's leaning against a filing cabinet, wearing a shirt that says "Let's Summon Demons," and looking like she wants to do exactly that. The two guys, Brian and Charlie, take their places next. Brian, a junior who's kind of like a cartoon scarecrow, and who got in trouble yesterday for wearing a "Trombones Do It In Seven Positions" T-shirt, sprawls out in the only chair in the room, with his trombone on his lap. Charlie, a senior who's kind of like a cartoon bear, hovers behind Colleen, looking like he'd rather be anywhere but here. I try not to think about what kind of cartoon character I look like, as I perch on the one inch of the folding table that isn't covered with sheet music, and pray it won't collapse under me.

Colleen pulls her blonde hair back into a perfect ponytail (how does every other girl know how to do that?) and puts her hands on her hips. Even off the podium, she oozes confidence. "Okay, guys, listen up," she says. "This was a tough decision. And no offense, Kat, I mean it."

Kat makes a sound halfway between a snort and a growl.

"And no offense, Brian, either."

He looks up from greasing his tuning slide. "Huh?"

Colleen continues. "But the drum majors talked with Mr. Coffman, and after yesterday, we think it's gonna be better for the trombone section if Charlie's section leader this year. Any questions, come talk to me, but this is how it's gonna be."

Charlie tries to blend into the bookcase behind him, and when that doesn't work, he gets really interested in retying his Nikes. Brian actually drops to his knees and shouts, "Hallelujah!"

Kat mutters, just loud enough so all of us can hear her, "It's not my fault some people can't march."

"But part of being a section leader is—"

"And it's not my fault some people are babies."

"Look, you know we talked about this last year, and if you can't—"

"God, don't start with me, Colleen."

This gets Charlie out of the bookcase. "Hey!"

But Colleen barely reacts at all. She says, all cool, like she's talking to an overtired toddler, "You can be as mad as you want. But we're not changing our minds." And then she leaves the room.

For a minute, no one moves. I'm not even sure I'm still breathing. Then Kat points a black-painted fingernail at Charlie, yells, "This is just because you're fucking her, isn't it?" and storms out of the room, knocking over three stacks of Sousa marches.

Charlie turns about 20 different shades of purple. Brian

stares at him for a minute and then smacks him on the back, saying, "Dude! You? And Colleen? Hell, yeah!"

Charlie glances at me and says, "Brian, shut up. Sorry, Meghan. And, yeah…I asked Colleen out last week. Okay? It's no big deal. And that's not why I'm section leader now, anyway. They decided Kat was a little too…"

"Bitchy?" Brian suggests.

"No."

"Bitch-tastic?"

"No."

"Bitch-ariffic?"

"No. Shut up, Brian. Sorry, Meg—"

"Bitch-alicious," I volunteer, interrupting Charlie. He and Brian stare at me for a minute. Then Brian snorts, and Charlie grins and says, "Yeah. That's it," and as small as it is, I feel like I've won a prize. A prize in making up new swear words, yeah, but still a prize.

"What about me?" Brian wants to know.

"What about you?" Charlie asks. "I'm not bitch-alicious. I'm a very nice person. Everyone thinks so. Right, Meghan?" He points at me with the business end of his slide, and I duck before I get a spit valve to the face.

"You're a very nice person," Charlie tells him, patting him on the shoulder. "But you're also a dumbass."

"And I'm not doing the head drum major."

"And you're not—" Charlie catches himself. "Jesus Christ, Brian. Sorry, Meghan."

"Does she call out commands when you're doing it?

Like"—he goes into falsetto—"'Oh, Charlie, mark time eight! Mark time eight!'"

"What the hell does that even mean?"

"It means Brian's a dumbass, but you knew that already," says Colleen, who's poked her head in again. "Come on out, guys. We're announcing the show." She takes Charlie's hand and they head into the band room together.

I stand up, then notice that Brian's slunk out of his chair and onto the floor. "You coming?" I ask.

"Nah, I think I'll stay here until Colleen forgets that ever happened. Maybe until graduation. Come and visit me sometimes, Meghan. Tell me happy stories of the outside world."

"Come on," I say, and when he reaches his hand up, in a mock-pathetic way, I take it, and pull him back up to standing. His hand is kind of sweaty, and kind of scratchy, and as soon as I realize I'm holding it, I drop it. "Let's find out what the show is."

Brian and I file out of the music library and take our places in the back of the band room. Kat's stomping out the classroom door with Maya. They catch sight of me over their shoulders, and when they glare at me, right before they slam the door, I can actually feel myself getting smaller.

Mr. Coffman steps up to the podium. He looks younger than most of the other teachers at DHS, like if you met him outside of school you'd get to call him by his first name, and he's got a big grin on his face. "Welcome to band camp!" he bellows. "I'm Mr. Coffman, and I'm your new band director. I've met most of you upperclassmen, and I'm looking forward to meeting all the newbies, too. I know Colleen and the other drum majors got you started with marching fundamentals yesterday. Today, we'll run through the music for this year's show, and then this afternoon we'll try to get the first song on the field. Go, Patriots!"

"Go, Patriots!" a few people mumble.

Mr. Coffman tries again. "Go, Patriots!"

"Go Patriots!" We all respond this time, and I'm not gonna lie, it feels good to yell like this, all together.

"But first," Mr. Coffman continues, "I want to talk a little about pride. I know those of you who've been in this band for a while have had a hard time in the last few years."

The "all together" feeling evaporates as I watch the juniors and seniors nod sagely, looking like they've all been through a war. I think about asking Brian what Mr. Coffman's talking about, but then I glance at Kat scowling at the other end of our row, and I think better of it.

"So I think the most important thing we need to do, before we can do anything else, is to get our pride back. Now we're gonna try something. When I ask you a question, I wanna hear you say, 'YES, SIR!' Got it?"

"YES, SIR!" say the kids who are awake enough to catch on.

"BAND! ARE YOU READY, BAND?"

This time we're all ready. "YES, SIR!"

"ARE YOU THE BEST MARCHING BAND?"

A little hesitation. "YES, SIR!"

"I CAN'T HEAR YOU. BAND! ARE YOU THE BEST MARCHING BAND?"

"YES, SIR!" we yell.

"Now, let's talk about this year's show. Now, everybody knows what MABC is, right?"

Even as a newbie, I know what MABC is (though I didn't know you pronounced it "mab-see" until now). It stands for Mid-Atlantic Band Championships, who run all the competitions. Half the trophies in the band room have the MABC insignia on them. Mondays in the fall were the only time I'd ever actually listen to the morning announcements, when they'd announce the competition scores and congratulate the band, and I'd think ahead to how cool it would be, hearing people congratulate me on the announcements next year. This year.

"Some schools like to game the system and keep up with the trends at MABC, and pick out shows they think the judges will like," he says, and then he fake-coughs "Carroll High," which cracks all the juniors and seniors up.

"But the trends are always changing. And I don't think our job is to keep up with trends," he says. "I think it's our job to entertain people. If we play a show we have fun with, then the audience is gonna have fun, too. So this year, we're gonna make 'em dance in the stands."

Which is all a long-winded way of saying we're playing old Motown songs. Old songs, but good songs. It's music to sing along into a hairbrush with, or make up choreography to at a sleepover. I keep trying to catch Dani's eye—didn't we even make up a dance to "I Want You Back" one time?—but she's busy chatting with Maya.

Colleen and the two junior drum majors, A.J. and Kenzie, pass out the music.

"God, Charlie, remember last year?" says Colleen, handing out copies of "I Want You Back" and "My Girl."

"At the Franklin competition?"

"OINK, OINK, OINK!" Charlie replies.

Brian joins in, putting his thumbs on either side of his head and waggling his fingers, all while singing the *Star Wars* theme.

A.J. comes by with "Signed, Sealed, Delivered." "Hey, you guys, who am I?" he asks, and yanks his pants up, sticks out his crotch, and stomps his feet.

Charlie and Brian crack up, and then they get up and start dancing, too.

"Last year at Franklin?" asks Kenzie, with her arms full of "Reach Out I'll Be There."

"You know it," Brian says, and they do a little fist bump.

For a second I think about joining in and pretending I'm part of the joke, too. Then I realize the only thing dumber than doing that dance would be doing it and not knowing why.

And now I'm wondering: didn't I join marching band

because I wanted to be a part of something?

#

At lunch, the band boosters bribe us with Joe Corbi's pizza, so they can win us over and convince us to sell pizza kits door to door, and it works, because pizza. I take a slice of cheese and a slice of pepperoni and head over to the clarinet section, hoping that if I get there before Maya, I'll be able to sit with Dani. By the time I get there, though, Dani's grabbing her purse and walking toward the door.

I call her name twice before she turns around.

"Sorry, Meghan," she says when she finally hears me. "Maya has her mom's car today, so we're doing clarinet bonding at the pizza place across the street."

"But…there's pizza here," I say stupidly, holding up my greasy paper plate like proof, or a peace offering. "The band boosters…brought us…pizza. And it's free."

Dani shrugs, looks a little guilty, and then looks back at Maya, who's standing at the band room door with some of the other clarinet girls, and their drummer boyfriends, waving her car keys.

Maya raises a perfect eyebrow at me, and then says to Dani, loud enough that everyone in the band can hear it, "She. Is. Not. Coming." Then she smiles and calls, "Come on, D., let's go!"

For a second, I actually think Dani will stay. But then she gives me a little wave, says, "We can talk later, okay?"

and then bolts out the door, leaving me behind.

I toss my plate into the trash can by the door, like that's the only reason I came over here in the first place, and then I sit back down in my sad little trombone corner and study the third trombone part for "My Girl." It's not that I don't have any friends. It's not that no one wants to eat lunch with me. I've got a lot of new and challenging music to learn. If I say that to myself enough, I know I'll believe it by the end of lunch. At least it might keep me from crying.

So let's see. Whole notes, huh? How many beats are they, again? Let's try counting them out slowly. One... two...three...four...

But then I start thinking about the trombone meeting that morning, and goofing around with Charlie and Brian. And how even while we were running through the music today, sometimes one of them would look at me and go, "Bitch-alicious," and we'd all crack up. So I get up and peek into the music library, where Charlie, Colleen, and A.J. are sprawled on the floor, and I say, praying I sound like a normal person, "Can I join you guys?"

"Yeah, make some room for us," says Brian, appearing next to me with two Cokes and two plates stacked high with pizza. Everybody scooches over without a word, and I follow Brian inside. Once we're joined by Kenzie and her boyfriend, a trumpet player named Dean, we're all kind of squished. But that's okay. It's kind of cozy.

Brian and Dean go back for seconds and thirds, and when the band boosters finally cut them off, they challenge each other to a Coke-chugging contest, which quickly turns into a belching contest, and while they're otherwise occupied, the rest of us talk. Well, they talk. And I listen. Colleen tells us about her summer job at the YMCA's kiddie sports camp, and then she makes Charlie show off how buff he is from mowing lawns all summer. Then Charlie, who by now has tied and re-tied his shoes about 50 times, changes the subject. "So Meghan," he says, "what about you?"

I guess he's asking what I've been doing all summer, which of course I totally don't want to answer, but then Brian goes, "Story time! Tell us the Meghan story!" and settles down in front of me, criss-cross applesauce, like I'm gonna read him *Don't Let The Pigeon Drive The Bus!* or something. Now they're all looking at me.

I say "um" a bunch of times. And then I end up telling them about how I started playing trombone. This is something you have to talk about a lot, when you're a girl who plays trombone, even these days. The short version is, it's my Gram's fault. Gram's a musical theater nut—she grew up outside New York City, and she used to go see all the big shows on Broadway. She moved down here to Maryland for college, and she was going to be a music teacher, but then she met Pop-Pop and they got married and had my mom, and they moved out to the Eastern Shore near Ocean City.

After Pop-Pop died, the year before I was born, Gram started making music again, playing rehearsal piano for a community theater group. And every summer, when we'd go out to visit her, she'd take us to see the latest show she'd worked on.

When I was six, the show was *The Music Man*, and I got obsessed with that song "Seventy-Six Trombones," and I spent the whole rest of the summer marching around the house going, "Hup, two, three, four!" and playing trombones made out of toilet paper tubes.

The part I never tell anyone is how what I really wanted to play was the trumpet. Trombones were fun when I was a little kid, but by fifth grade, I knew trumpets were loud and cool and in charge, and that's what I wanted to be. But I guess everyone else in fifth grade beginning band had the same idea, so our director said the Larger Kids who'd signed up for trumpet would have to move to the larger brass instruments. So Nicky Zukosky got switched to tuba, and I got switched to trombone.

I was pissed at first. Just because I liked "Seventy-Six Trombones" when I was six, didn't mean I wanted to play trombone when I was 10. I mean, when I was seven, Gram took me to see *The Sound of Music*, and I was obsessed all summer with "Do-Re-Mi," but you didn't see me wanting to wear curtains and hide from the Nazis, either. And who ever heard of girls playing the trombone, anyway? I spent the whole fall worrying that everyone was going to make fun of me. And a few kids did. Even Dani, once or twice.

But I kept playing. And it turned out that, more often than not, I could play the right notes at the right time. My mom said, "You must get it from your Gram," and I hoped she was right.

Over Christmas that year, we went to visit Gram, and on Christmas afternoon, while she and I were playing my new Clue game, she asked me how band was going. Maybe I was overtired, but I burst into tears and started crying about how I didn't wanna play a boy instrument, and trombones were stupid, and it wasn't fair. Gram put down her cards and hugged me, and I let her, even though I was ten years old and way too big for hugs anymore.

When I calmed down a little, she told me some stories about the all-women big bands in the '30s and '40s, and Melba Liston, who played trombone with all the stars back then and even had her own band for a while. And the next day, when she took me to see *The Nutcracker*, we leaned over the pit while the musicians warmed up, and we saw a woman playing the trombone, just like me. When the woman caught me bouncing and pointing, she smiled and waved back. "This is my granddaughter," Gram called to her. "She just picked up the trombone herself. She's going to be a star."

I blushed, and tried to hide behind my hair, but the lady said, "Good for you! Show those boys how it's done." And she smiled again, and winked at me, and Gram squeezed my hand.

And after that, I didn't care about people teasing me anymore. I actually started to think playing trombone was pretty cool. And I didn't even think about switching back to trumpet.

I give Brian and everybody the Cliff's Notes version of the story, and they're all so nice listening to me that I get up the courage to ask them some questions, about MABC, and competitions, and what Mr. Coffman was talking about earlier, about pride, and what happened during the last few years.

"Oh, no," Charlie groans. "You want the Mr. K. story."

"It's a tragic tale of woe," says Brian. "Someday I'm going to learn to play the banjo so I can turn it into a folk ballad."

"I'm gonna tell the story," Charlie says, "and no one's going to sing."

So Charlie tells me about Mr. K., who directed the band for the last 20 years, and just retired this spring. Back in the day, according to Charlie, the band used to win first place trophies all the time. Then, about five years ago, things started going downhill. "That's when he stopped letting freshmen do marching band. It was the worst class ever," Charlie says.

"Even worse than yours, Meghan," Brian interrupts. "I mean, no offense, but you guys couldn't even march yesterday."

"Neither could you, last year," says Charlie.

"Oh, and you could?" Colleen asks, and Charlie thwaps her.

"But that's not the point," Charlie continues. "The point is four years ago, they caught the whole freshman class smoking weed on the band trip to Florida. So the band boosters said no more band trips, and he got mad, and he said no more freshmen in marching band, and then the boosters got mad, and they made him stay on through last year to help find someone new."

"The band boosters could do that?" I ask. The freshman band boosters could barely get a bake sale together.

"The band boosters can do anything. Dean's mom is president this year," Kenzie says, "and she's a beast."

"She is," Dean agrees. "Just like you."

Kenzie does a little fake growl, and Dean kisses her. I can see both of their tongues. It's gross.

"Where'd they get all the weed?" I ask, changing the subject.

Charlie shrugs. "You know drummers."

"It wasn't weed, though," A.J. butts in. "And it wasn't four years ago. It was coke, five years ago, on the band trip to Toronto."

"No way, man," says Dean, "you've got it all wrong. It was six years ago, on the band trip to Phoenix, and Mr. K got some drum major drunk on wine coolers, and the band boosters walked in while he was doing her in the bathtub."

"What?"

"My cousin told me. The girl got pregnant, and he said the kid wasn't his, so she started stalking him. And then his wife kicked him out, and now he drives an Uber on the weekend to pay for child support."

"No way," Brian says. "That's nuts."

"I know," Charlie agrees.

"Because we all know Mr. K. works weekends as a stripper."

Brian smirks as everyone screams and covers their eyes.

"Meghan, what do you think?"

Brian's question takes me by surprise. I almost thought they'd all forgotten I was here. I tell him the only thing I know for sure at the moment: "I think my head hurts."

Then a band booster pops in with a plate full of "dessert pizza"—pizza dough topped with pie filling and chocolate sauce—and pretty soon my stomach hurts, too. Charlie catches me wincing a little, with my hand over my stomach, and says, "You look like you wanna die."

"I kinda do," I say.

And everybody raises their dessert pizza like a toast, and Charlie says, "Welcome to marching band, Meghan."

CHAPTER FOUR

It's two minutes before the first day of school starts, and I'm all alone in the band hallway.

Okay, I'm not alone. Half the band is here, waiting for Mr. Coffman to show up and unlock the door. Way back in June, Dani and I had made plans to meet in the band hallway before school, so we could compare classes one more time, and check out each other's new outfits, and basically give each other some kind of support, like friends are supposed to do. But that was before she blew me off for Maya and the other clarinets.

Maybe I'm jealous because my section's idea of bonding is Brian making jokes about Charlie's sex life until Charlie tries to punch him.

Or maybe I'm jealous because it feels like I've lost my best friend.

Dani finally shows up just after the first bell rings, with Maya, some other clarinet girls, and—eep—Kat, clutching venti coffee cups. Dani doesn't even drink coffee. At least, she didn't used to.

I catch her eye and wave to her. She tries to pretend she doesn't see me. I try even harder to pretend it doesn't hurt.

"Move!" Kat shoves me, and everyone else in her path, out of the way as she barrels toward the band room door.

And with that, the second bell rings. The first day of school has begun.

First period is band, and we spend it marching on the field so we can all be sweaty and smelly for the rest of the day. Kat yells at me four times for being out of step, three times for not keeping my horn parallel to the ground, twice for being slow to snap from parade rest to attention, and once for just "making everyone look bad." When we line up to march back to the classroom, Brian gives me an awkward shoulder pat and says, "It'll get easier. I mean, probably." He leaves his hand there until we're called to attention.

That time, Kat yells at both of us.

I don't see Dani again until French class. She and I started French together last year, thinking it would be the most sophisticated language we could learn, and then we spent all year watching videos about a singing, dancing pineapple. She's already in the room when I get there, and I take the empty desk on her left.

"Hey, Dani, long time no see." I'm trying to sound casual, but my voice shakes when I say her name.

"Um." She sounds exactly like Maya when she says it. Without even looking at me, she whips out her lipstick and a compact and starts touching up her makeup. Her lipstick is the same dark red as Maya's, and it looks awful on her. "Um. I don't think we're supposed to be talking right now."

I check the front of the room. Madame Boudreau is

nowhere in sight. She usually doesn't show until five minutes after the bell. "Class hasn't started yet."

"No." Dani sighs, one of those "the weight of the world is on my shoulders and I'm surrounded by idiots" sighs she's gotten so good at over the last year or so. "I mean… look, Maya is, like, really upset about what you did to Kat."

"About what?" I can't believe what I'm hearing.

"You know. Getting her in trouble with Colleen? Making her step down as section leader? Just so Colleen's boyfriend could take over?"

"But I didn't do anything."

Dani shuts me up with a wave of her manicured hand. "Everybody's mad," she says. "No one's supposed to talk to you. That's what Maya said."

I think about the breakfast I gobbled down a few hours before, and I swear there's a strawberry Pop-Tart making its way up from my stomach to the back of my throat.

"What are you talking about?" I can barely get the words out.

"Maya and Kat have been best friends since, like, sixth grade," she says.

"So have we," I manage to reply.

She has the decency to look a little guilty. Just a little. And then Madame Boudreau runs in and tells us to practice introducing ourselves to our neighbors while she gets a video ready.

Dani twists her entire body so she's facing the guy on her right. Fine. Whatever.

I turn to the girl on my left. *"Bonjour. Je m'appelle Meghan Riggins. Tu t'appelles comment?"*

She doesn't even look up from the phone she's tapping on. *"Je m'appelle Becca Wheeler,"* she says. "Girl, you smell like a dead cow."

Merde.

French is so bad I'm actually excited to get out of there and onto English class. That is, until Ms. Ramos gets to my name on her attendance sheet and asks the question I dread every year: "Meghan Riggins? Are you Nina's sister?" Great. It's not too often I get one of Nina's old teachers, but whenever I do, they usually spend the whole year wondering why I'm not living up to my sister's potential. It's disappointing and embarrassing for everyone involved, but I'm the only one whose grades end up suffering. I mumble something noncommittal, and luckily, Ms. Ramos is less interested in talking to me and more interested in handing out a 10-page list of rules and regulations. She spends most of the period giving us a lecture on how we're not freshmen anymore, we're *young adults*—and then she hands out copies of a book about talking bunnies.

At lunch time, I'm still freaking out about what Dani said in French class. After I buy my lunch, I stand there, frozen at the end of the lunch line. There's plenty of kids I know, and even some girls I'm kind of friendly with, but I keep hearing Dani in my head: "No one's supposed to talk to you." No one in the clarinet section? No one in band? No one in the whole school?

Finally, I grab a chair at the nearest empty table. I leave *Watership Down* open next to me, and spend a minute or two pretending to furrow my brow at it, like I'm only alone because I have So Much Serious Work To Do—and then Rachel Reznik appears, with her lunch bag and her own copy of *Watership Down* in hand. "Meghan, right? Mind if I join you?"

Rachel and I have gone to school together since sixth grade, but we've never been in the same class. Dani and I were always around the same (low) level of popularity as her and her friends, but since we were band nerds and they were art nerds, we never really talked to each other. Maybe she hasn't heard the news yet, that no one's supposed to talk to me. Maybe band nerd rules don't apply to art nerds.

Maybe I should get out of my head, and be polite, and actually say something to her.

"Hey, Rachel. How was your summer?"

Not a bad start. Right?

"It was fabulous," Rachel says. "I made a stop-motion animation film about Rosh Hashanah."

And I'm speechless again, because there's absolutely no way I can follow that, so I'm almost relieved when the guys at the next table yell, "Fight!" and start lobbing mashed potatoes across the room.

Rachel and I take cover under our table. "What did you do?" she asks.

D'oh. Should I go with, "My best friend ditched me for her section leader"?

I stick with the shortest answer: "I went to band camp."

"Oh, yeah, you're in band. What do you play?"

"Trombone," I say, and wait for the usual reaction.

Instead, Rachel says, "My little brother Jonah plays trombone, too. He's a freshman. He was thinking about doing marching band next year, but then one of his friends told him they make all the new kids march around with their underwear on their heads."

"Wow," I say, "I guess band camp *could* have been even worse."

She pokes her head up from under the table. "I think we're safe now."

I poke my head up, too, and end up with mashed potatoes in my hair. Rachel giggles, but only a little.

"Sorry," she says, reaching over with a napkin to get it out.

"Thanks." I'm honestly surprised that she's helping me out. If Dani were here, she would've just laughed at me.

Then Rachel slams her hand on the table. "You're the one that dumb girl was talking about in my video production class!"

"What?"

"Some dumb girl. I think she's in marching band—some girl who plays clarinet? She said no one was supposed to talk to this trombone girl, because she got this other trombone girl in trouble or something. Nobody was paying attention. It's like, if someone deletes my work in video production, I don't go into the band room and tell the drummers to ostracize her. Right?"

"Right?"

"Right." She leans over with her napkin again and gets the last bit of potato out of my hair. "I don't care what some dumb girl is saying about you. Give it a day or two and no one else will, either."

"Thanks," I say, and suddenly, I'm feeling better than I have all day.

CHAPTER FIVE

It would be cool to celebrate surviving the first week of school by staying home in my pajamas and pretending to read for English while really watching TV with Ellie. But instead I get to spend it…at school. With the marching band. At our first football game. It's hard to remember that a few months ago, this was kind of my dream.

We've got one and a half songs on the field so far, so we're going to march through "I Want You Back" and then stay in the ending formation to play "My Girl." We run through both songs in the band room, and then we split up to change into our uniforms—guys in the band locker room, girls in the chorus room across the hall.

During band camp, the band boosters measured us all for uniforms and hats (meaning they found out our sizes and then tried to find band uniforms and hats we might be able to fit into, if we were lucky), and now we all carry our ugly grey garment bags to the chorus room, where Colleen and Kenzie talk us through the uniforms:

1. The stuff we're supposed to bring from home. A long-sleeved white dress shirt, plain black dress socks, and the "marching band shoes": black dress shoes we were supposed to special-order from a marching band supply

warehouse or something. Mine haven't arrived yet, because the order got buried underneath a bunch of Swarthmore paraphernalia and Ellie's soccer schedule, and I didn't find it or—let's be honest—remember it until a few days ago. I'm wearing a pair of my dad's black dress shoes, with a paper towel stuffed in at each toe, because my feet may be big for a girl, but they're still not as big as his.

2. The jacket. It's navy blue, with fancy gold piping all over it. It comes with a gold chain that fastens between two buttonholes near the bottom.

3. The dickey (cue Brian snickering here). A ruffly piece of fabric that buttons onto the dress shirt. It's like the marching band version of a tuxedo t-shirt, and just as classy.

4. The cummerbund. And the flag. As in, "capture the." As in, "what the hell." The flag goes on the right side of the cummerbund, centered on the yellow (gold) stripe on the right side of the pants.

5. Oh, yeah, the pants. They're the same blue as the jacket, and except for the yellow (gold) stripes on either side, they're really not too bad. The hat, on the other hand...

6. The hat. It's blue and shiny, with a gold squiggly

military-type design in the center. And at the top, front and center, goes a bright yellow feathery plume.

7. Also, we have to wear white gloves.

I'm not sure what the overall effect of the uniform is supposed to be, but by the time I have the whole thing on the way Colleen wants it, I look a lot like Cookie Monster. Cookie Monster with a trombone.

In the parking lot outside the band room, the drummers are pounding out our marching cadence, the trumpets are challenging each other to see how loud and high they can play, and the newbie flutes are freaking because no one told them they'd have to put their hair up inside their hats. Dani catches my eye from across the room and gives me the tiniest of waves. We didn't talk at all on Tuesday or Wednesday, but by yesterday, she was back to saying hi to me in French class. And today, when Madame Boudreau had us doing worksheets, Dani asked me how to conjugate the verb *aller*. Does this mean we're friends again? Or does it mean Maya wasn't watching, and Dani's even worse at French than I am?

My spot in the parade formation is between Brian and Nicky Zukosky the sousaphone player. Brian says, "Man, I remember my first football game. Hey, Charlie, remember last year? When we played Carroll?" He picks up an air trombone, almost sending his real trombone clattering to the ground, and sings something that sounds like a mix between the Harry Potter theme and a jingle from some old Lego commercial. I try to ignore him and start wondering why I can still remember the Lego ad, when I've never played with a single Lego in my life.

Colleen claps her hands four times and bellows, "Band, parade rest!" I stick my feet shoulder-width apart, and place my gloved hands on top of my trombone.

Colleen continues, "Band, hut-ten-hut!" We're supposed to respond by snapping our feet together, bringing our horns up to attention, and yelling, "Patriots!" all at the same time. I've been practicing at home, but it's different when I don't know it's coming. My trombone goes up, but my feet are about half a second late, and while I'm freaking out about that, I forget to yell, "Patriots!" and my brain decides to make up for that by having me yell it at the top of my lungs after everyone else is finished. This is why, back in elementary school on field day, all the other kids used to fight over who got to race me in the 50-yard dash.

Since I'm at attention, I'm not allowed to move, no matter how much I'd like to turn around and run right home. Out of the corner of my left eye, past Brian and Charlie, I see Kat, and I can almost hear her thinking out all the different ways she's gonna yell at me as soon as she gets the chance.

"Band! Horns up!" Colleen blows her whistle three times, and we snap our horns up. At least I get this part right.

"Mark time, march!"

"Pop, left, right, left, right," I mutter under my breath, hoping my feet are listening, and we're off. We march through the school parking lot, past the band boosters in their blue and gold sweatshirts, waving noisemakers and cheering for their kids, and across the street to the football field. The iron fence around the field is decorated with blue and yellow hand-painted signs, and the stands are packed with kids from school, parents, and local people with no lives. Everyone cheers when we enter the field, and I find myself getting caught up in it, and even getting a little excited again, as we file up to our reserved bleachers.

"Stay in your sections, everybody," Colleen calls. "Victory March in five."

Up in the press booth, the guys from Cable 10 are blathering about the DHS football team, and how some kid who once threw a baseball bat at me in elementary school is going to lead them all to victory. Two senior cheerleaders stand in front of the field entrance, holding a hand-painted banner that says, "GO PATRIOT'S," and the team crashes through it, hopefully before too many people can read it. Colleen blows the whistle four times, and we launch into the victory march.

I don't pay much attention to the game. Unlike Ellie, I don't care about sports—not because I'm intellectually superior, like Nina, but more because I'm an uncoordinated klutz. Football always seems to me like an excuse for testosterone freaks to beat each other up without getting suspended from school. Luckily for the band, it also involves a hell of a lot of time when the teams are standing around like idiots, and when that happens, it's our job to step up and keep the crowd from dying of boredom. We play "Don't Stop Believin'" so many times in the first half alone that soon I don't even need to look at the music in my flip folder any more. It's not that big of an accomplishment—the third trombone part is mostly whole notes—but I feel good about it.

Whenever Colleen, A.J., and Kenzie get tired of waving their arms around, the cheerleaders step up and yell at us:

"Patriots got the power! Patriots got the heat! Patriots got the spirit to knock you off your feet!"

I think about the giant clown shoes I'm wearing and realize there's a very real possibility of my being knocked off my feet. I don't even wanna think about what Kat will do if that happens.

"More power to the hour! More bounce to the ounce! When you catch that Patriot spirit, it's gonna knock you out!"

Why are all of the cheers about falling down?

That last cheer is still going through my head at halftime, and I'm cursing my stupid clown shoes as we stumble out of the bleachers onto the track, into parade formation.

"Prayer time," Charlie announces, and the three of us huddle up. I wonder for a second if Charlie's gonna whip out a rosary or something, but instead he folds his hands and says, "God is great, God is good, trombones rock this neighborhood. 'Low brass kicks ass' on three."

We put our hands in the middle, and he counts, "One, two, three."

"Low brass kicks ass!" we yell.

All around us, the other sections are saying their own cheers. The saxophones and flutes have choreography. The trumpets do a Tarzan yell. The drummers throw their sticks at each other, and they somehow manage to pick them all up in time to start the cadence.

"Now, please welcome your Dulaney High School Marching Patriots!" they announce from the press box as we march our way to chart zero. "The Marching Patriots are directed by Matthew Coffman, with drum majors senior Colleen Lalley, and juniors A.J. Renoud and Kenzie Hillman. This year, the band's show is called 'Motown Magic.'"

"Oversell much?" Brian mutters, and I try not to laugh.

"Drum majors, is the band ready?"

Colleen salutes from her podium. A.J. and Kenzie, on either side of her, do the same. Then Colleen claps and calls us to attention, and we're off.

"I Want You Back" goes fine. It's a simple drill, even for us idiot newbies. When it's over, we're supposed to freeze in formation and play "My Girl." And I know we're supposed to freeze in formation and play "My Girl." I really do. Mentally, I mean. But my feet get all excited and distracted, and my left foot launches out in front of me, into the "My Girl" drill. As soon as my foot swings out, I catch myself, and I try to swing it back, but my clown shoe catches on the hem of my stupid blue and gold pants, and I fall on my face.

I'm pretty sure the rest of the band starts playing anyway, and maybe I even put my trombone back together (because, of course, the outer slide has fallen off, and when I bend down to pick it up, I knock my flip folder off my lyre) and squeak out a few notes, but my mind is too busy dying of embarrassment to notice what my body is doing. We march off the field, and Brian can't even look at me, he's trying so hard not to laugh.

The way I see it, I have three choices right now:

1. Go running to my mommy and daddy, who both texted me a few hours ago that they were working late but hoping to make the game by halftime.

2. Go running to Dani, who's still the closest thing to a friend I've got, and make her hide out with me under the bleachers for the rest of the game.

3. Go running out of the stadium for good. Preferably into traffic.

So as soon as we make it back to the stands, and Colleen dismisses us for our third-quarter break, I make my way over to the clarinet section. Maybe we're not best friends anymore—maybe we're not even friends anymore, a voice in my head says, but I squash that thought as soon as it appears—but those years we were best friends have gotta count for something. I grab Dani, not even caring that she's in the middle of a conversation with Maya, and say, "I'm gonna crawl under the stands and hide there until everyone else goes home, and I kind of need you to come with me."

She looks pained. "We're gonna get something to eat. Just the clarinets."

The worst part is, her answer actually surprises me.

I stumble down the stairs anyway. Maybe I'll stay there forever. As soon as I get under the bleachers, though, I realize I have no business being there. Kids are standing around smoking and drinking and feeling each other up like half the teachers in our school aren't sitting right above them. Becca Wheeler and some other girls from French class notice me, smirk at my band uniform, and then whisper to each other and crack up.

I step back quickly, hoping to find an escape route. Instead, I bump into a couple fused together like a two-headed monster. It's Charlie and Colleen, and he's got his tongue down her throat and both of his hands under her dickey. "Sorry," I mumble, and I hightail it back to the safety of the upper world. I may be a Young Adult in English class, but I'm not ready for this yet.

"Hey, Meghan!" someone calls when I reach the surface.

I don't answer at first. I don't even look up from my shoes. I figure it's someone who wants to congratulate me on making an ass out of myself on the field, and I don't think I can deal with that right now.

"Meghan!" the voice repeats. "Great job!"

It doesn't sound sarcastic, so I look up. It's Rachel Reznik, and I'm guessing the guy next to her is her brother. He's a little bit taller than her, but he's got the same curly dark brown hair (minus the blue streaks she's added to hers), and big brown eyes behind his glasses, and his T-shirt says something about dragons thinking people taste good with ketchup. He's kind of cute. You know. For a freshman.

"Jonah, Meghan," Rachel says, waving a hand back and forth between us, "meet each other."

"You guys sounded awesome," Jonah says.

"Thanks," I say, once I remember that's what you say when someone says something nice to you.

"You're welcome," he says. "So, who fell down?"

I look back at the band section, where people are starting to gather again.. "Um...I gotta get back in the stands. See you guys later."

#

We lose the game, and Kat can barely wait until we're changing in the chorus room to start reaming me out in front of all the other girls. "You made all of us look like shit out there," she starts, and I can only imagine how much more fun it's gonna get from here, before Colleen says, loud enough to cut through all the chatter in the chorus room, "Kat. Shut. The. Fuck. Up."

49

Kat slaps her, and everyone in the entire room gasps in unison.

Colleen just stares her down. And even though Kat's six feet tall and fully clothed, and Colleen's barely 5'6" and in her underwear (which, by the way, has cartoon monkeys all over it), Kat retreats.

"Listen up, ladies!" Colleen yells. "Any of you who were never a newbie, raise your hands right now."

No one moves a muscle.

"That's what I thought. At ease."

I'm gathering up my garment bag and backpack when Colleen comes over to me and puts her hand on my shoulder. She's still in her monkey underwear.

"Hey," she says. "Everyone knows Kat was out of line then. And if she gives you any more crap, you tell me, or you tell Charlie. And you tell her to stuff it. Got it?"

"Got it," I repeat, though I'm not sure I do. And it's gonna be hard to tell Colleen or Charlie anything until I shake off the image of them under the bleachers.

I don't even bother going back to the band room once I'm dressed. I'm pretty sure my trombone and I aren't on speaking terms right now, so it can stay in the locker room for the rest of the weekend.

Outside in the parking lot, other kids call to each other about getting rides to Denny's, or to the field party out in back of so-and-so's house. I catch sight of Dani getting into Maya's car, and then Mom and Ellie pull up in our minivan.

"Hi, honey," Mom says as I open the car door. "Nice job out there! The band sounded great!"

"Who fell down?" Ellie wants to know.

"Some guy named Brian," I say. "I'm really beat, okay? Let's get home."

And when I get home? I message Rachel.

Me: Hey. Thanks for not mocking me at the game today.

Rachel: Meghan!!

Rachel: Dude!! I'm so glad you msged me.

Rachel: Jonah hasn't shut up all night about the marching band.

Rachel has added Jonah to the conversation.

Jonah: whut

Rachel: Jonah! It's your trombone heroine!

. . .

. . .

Rachel: Jonah just threw a paper plate in my face.

Me: What?

Rachel: Sorry. Watching Plan 9 from Outer Space over here, and shit just got real. Hang on a second.

. . .

. . .

Jonah: OW

Rachel: YOU SEE? YOUR STUPID MINDS! STUPID! STUPID!

Jonah: CAN YOUR HEART STAND THE

SHOCKING FACTS ABOUT MY KICKING YOUR ASS????

Me: ??????

Rachel: If you're not too wiped from the game, you should come over. The movie's only halfway over, and we'll catch you up on what you've missed.

Jonah: Nothing. You've missed nothing.

Jonah: And it's been EPIC.

Rachel: Seriously. I'd love to see you.

Rachel: Jonah would, too.

Rachel: OW. HE DID IT AGAIN.

\#

The whole Reznik family shows up at my house to pick me up. I can't think of the last time everyone in my family was in the same place, at least not since we visited Gram in the summer. Maybe Mr. and Mrs. Reznik aren't perfect, either, but they laugh a lot, and they sing along with the Beatles station in the car. I like them immediately.

Rachel's parents want to know all about how the show went tonight, and I know I'll tell Rachel the real story later, but for now, with Jonah listening, I make it sound like it kicked ass. I mean, he's a freshman. He's probably too young to handle the truth yet.

I change the subject as soon as I can, though, and that's how I spend the rest of the ride back to their place watching Rachel and Jonah reenact the entire script of *Plan*

9 from Outer Space. Apparently, Jonah's on some quest to watch the top 50 worst movies ever made, as ranked by some weirdo on the internet, and Plan 9 is so bad, it switches from day to night in the middle of every scene, and all the flying saucers in the movie are played by paper plates on strings. "Okay," I say, "I need to see this now." Rachel and Jonah agree.

When we get to the Rezniks' house, Rachel and Jonah show me *Plan 9*, which is even worse than it sounded, and then Rachel's Rosh Hashanah movie. It turns out Rachel's obsessed with those creepy old stop-motion Christmas specials, like *Rudolph the Red-Nosed Reindeer* and *Santa Claus Is Comin' To Town*, but she's decided that Christians shouldn't hog all the fun or the psychological scarring, so she's making her own films about the Jewish holidays. The three of us stay up most of the night, hanging out in the basement, watching movies and working on the Godzilla parody Rachel's doing for Sukkot. ("If the point of a holiday is that you build a house," Rachel explains, "then the point of the movie is to have a monster smash that house.") Jonah donates a Godzilla figure and a few other old toys to the cause, and spends most of the night telling me dumb jokes, stacking a pyramid of empty Diet Coke cans (Godzilla crashes into that, too), and actually excusing himself when he burps. He may be a freshman, but he's a huge improvement over most of the other guys I know.

By about three in the morning, Rachel's decision to put a David Bowie song on her soundtrack has led to our watching *Labyrinth*, a weird '80s fantasy movie. We've put Jonah in charge of making more popcorn, because we're older and we say so. (Somehow, that works.) On the TV, David Bowie, as the Goblin King, is dancing in his castle, throwing a baby around and singing about how it has the power of voodoo, whatever that means, and Rachel says, "You know, when you think about it, this whole movie is, like, a big ode to David Bowie's crotch."

"Ew!" I yelp. But then I look back at the TV screen during an unfortunate close-up. "Oh, my God. I think you're right."

We're cracking up (into pillows, so we won't wake Mr. and Mrs. Reznik), when Jonah comes back. "Hey, guys." He raises his eyebrows at us. "What's so funny?"

"Nothing," Rachel manages to say between giggles.

"You know," he says, "I read somewhere that they hid pictures of that guy's face all over the set."

"Better his face than something else," I say before I can stop myself, and Rachel and I lose it again.

Jonah shakes his head. "I'm going to bed. 'Night, guys. Nice having you here, Meghan. Pleasant dreams." And he bolts up the stairs.

As soon as he's out of sight, Rachel starts giggling again.

"What's so funny?" I ask, sounding like her brother.

"'Pleasant dreams, Meghan,'" she says in a ridiculous voice, and then she has to hide her face in her pillow again.

I have no idea what she's laughing about, but it's three in the morning, and we've been up all night watching movies, and right now on the TV there's a dead rock star wearing a codpiece and dancing with Muppets. I give up and grab my pillow, too.

#

At breakfast—it's more like lunch, since we all slept way too late—Rachel's parents start quizzing me about marching band.

I surprise myself by talking it up like it's the greatest thing since David Bowie's crotch.

"Well, I can't tell you how glad I am to hear that," Mrs. Reznik says, "because I got an email from Ms. Lozaro and Mr. Coffman this morning, and it seems like they've got a space for Jonah, starting Monday."

Jonah almost chokes on a mouthful of cereal. "What?"

"Mr. Coffman said there'd been some kind of issue with one of the trombones, and he needed to replace them with a freshman."

And now I'm choking internally, because this can only mean one thing: Kat's out.

Mrs. Reznik's still going. "And he asked Ms. Lozaro to recommend one, and she picked you! Isn't that fantastic? Here, let me find the email."

Mrs. Reznik finds it on her phone and then starts reading what Ms. Lozaro said, about Jonah being a quick study and an excellent player.

Jonah blushes and buries his head in his cereal bowl, but

I can tell he's smiling.

"I guess I'll see you Monday morning," I say to him. "Congratulations."

Jonah's smile gets bigger. Mine does, too.

CHAPTER SIX

Monday morning, no surprise, Brian and Dean are in front of the band room, each blabbing their own version of what happened Friday night to anyone who will listen. Never mind that neither of them were in the chorus room when it happened.

Brian: "So then Colleen's like, 'The fuck did you just say?' and then Kat grabs her and puts her in a headlock—"

Dean: "Nah, man, Kat takes off her bra and tries strangling Colleen with it, and then Colleen's like—"

Brian: "Dude, yeah, that's exactly it, then Colleen takes off her bra, and then—"

"Oh, my fucking God, assholes," Colleen groans, pushing then gently aside so she can unlock the band room door. "Shut up and sit down and put your dicks back in your pants. In reverse order, please."

"Sorry, Meghan," says Charlie, following close behind her.

Brian and Dean have the decency to look embarrassed, and so do the few kids who were actually listening to them. But as we follow Colleen into the band room, Brian grabs my arm and whispers to me, "So, I did get most of that right, didn't I? I mean, no offense, but when Danny said Kat was yelling at a newbie, I figured it was you."

I sigh. "Yeah, it was me. But everyone kept their clothes on." I figure Brian doesn't need to know about the monkey underwear. "So, Kat's really out?"

Brian leans closer to me, so his breath tickles my ear and my spit curls. It's...honestly not the most terrible thing I've ever felt. "Even worse," he says. "She's been demoted to Tupperware." Still holding my arm, he points it towards the drums in the back of the room. Kat's standing with them, holding a glockenspiel and glowering.

"Tupperware?"

"You know, the instruments in the pit, up by the drum majors. The kids who don't march, they just bang on, like, pots and pans."

I picture Kat as a bratty toddler, sitting in her diaper on her kitchen floor, smashing her parents' Tupperware with a wooden spoon. It wouldn't surprise me if I were imagining something 100% accurate.

With a start, I realize Brian hasn't let go of my arm yet.

"We'd better go sit down," I say, and I untangle myself and head for our seats. Brian takes Kat's old spot on Charlie's right, I sit on Brian's right, and then a dazed-looking Jonah wanders into the classroom, carrying his trombone case and wearing a T-shirt that says, "Keep Circulating The URL."

"Jonah! Over here!" I call. A few people who aren't Jonah turn and look at me. Does my voice always sound that loud and weird? Jonah flashes me a gigantic, grateful grin and lopes over to the seat on my right.

"You're Jonah? Hey, man, I'm Charlie. I'm the section leader." Charlie holds his hand out for a complicated bro handshake, but Jonah takes it and shakes it like a normal person. It's kind of cute.

"New guy," Brian says by way of greeting, his voice dripping with lack of enthusiasm.

"Old...guy," Jonah responds.

Charlie helps out. "That's Brian, and that's Meghan."

"Oh, Meghan and I go way back," Jonah says. "We celebrated Sukkot together."

Charlie raises his eyebrows.

"I'm friends with his sister," I explain.

"So you're taking over for Kat?" Brian asks. "A week before our first competition?"

"I...guess?" Jonah says. "Mr. Coffman just asked me to —"

"Have you ever marched before?"

"He's staying after school with me and Colleen so we can practice with him," Charlie says.

Brian makes a face of mock-horror, and suddenly he looks more like himself than he has in the last few minutes. "Look, what you and Colleen do in your private time is one thing, but bringing this poor, innocent little kid into your twisted sex life—"

"I'm not a poor, innocent little kid," Jonah protests, sounding exactly like one.

Before Brian can respond, Mr. Coffman steps up to the podium. "BAND! ARE YOU READY, BAND?"

"YES, SIR!" we chorus.

Jonah nudges me. "What was that?" he whispers.

"It's a thing," I say, feeling very wise. "Just go with it."

#

Once even Brian has to admit that Jonah's not a total disaster at putting one foot in front of the other, the big drama of the week is signing up for buses. The band takes three buses when we have to travel for a competition, and we sign up for them on a first-come, first-serve basis. Every clique has a different strategy for getting on the "right bus," whatever that means. Before Colleen even posts the sign-up sheets, she's signed up herself, Charlie, Kenzie, Dean, and A.J. for bus one. Maya protests, "No fair, that's totally cheating!" and then signs up the entire clarinet section for bus two. Then some of the senior drummers barge into the room and tear the bus three sign-up sheet off the wall so they can pass it around to their friends.

I watch all of this from my trombone locker. The whole thing's idiotic, I know. The competition's in the next county over, less than an hour away, so who cares what bus you end up on? But still, I kind of wish I had a reason to be fighting in the crowd. Someone I wanted to spend the bus ride with.

On my way out of the locker room, I bump into Dani on her way in.

"Hey," she mumbles, looking past me at Nicky Zukosky's sousaphone locker.

Part of me knows she's only saying hi because Maya isn't in the room. But it's the rest of me—the stupid, stupid rest of me—that decides to talk. "Hey. Did you sign up for a bus yet?"

Dani winces, still staring at the locker. "Really, Meghan? After what you did to Kat?"

After...what I did to Kat? I'm too mad to think of any way to respond, so I slink back to my seat alone, and bury myself in my music stand. But then Brian takes his seat next to me, and the first words out of his mouth are, "Hey, Meghan, I signed you up for bus one so you can ride with me and Charlie."

I'm surprised, and I guess it shows on my face, because he continues, "You didn't already sign up for another bus, did you? Aw, man. Well, you'll have to switch over. The low brass bus is always the best bus. I'm in charge of the singalongs."

"I thought they made a rule last year that you weren't allowed to sing on the bus anymore," Charlie says.

"That was last year," says Brian. "It's a whole new year, with a whole new crop of band booster chaperones to annoy. Do you know 'Bohemian Rhapsody,' Meghan?"

"What about 'Bohemian Rhapsody'?" Jonah asks, settling into his seat.

"Bus one singalong," Brian says.

"Hey, I signed up for bus one," Jonah says. "I saw all

you guys were on it, and I figured it was the place to be."

"Oh, it's the place to be, all right," says Brian.

"The place to be if you want a headache," Charlie mutters. "I don't know why Colleen signed us up for it."

"Because there's nothing hotter than my Freddie Mercury impression."

I let Brian and Charlie's banter wash over me, and I laugh, because suddenly I'm feeling better again. And because maybe Dani's watching

#

Things to bring on marching band bus trips:

1. Powerful headphones. Especially if you end up on the same bus as the trumpets, who like to scream a lot, or the drummers, who can't help banging on things, or Brian, who is, well, Brian.

2. A sleep mask. Or, if you're like me, and you're pretty much against buying anything with the word "Princess" on it, bring a hoodie or something to cover your eyes. Because if your eyes are closed, you'll look like you're asleep. And if you look like you're asleep, then you won't have to talk to the people who think if someone looks sad and lonely, you should ask them over and over again why they look so sad, why they never talk, and why they have no friends.

3. A friend.

Things I actually bring on my first marching band bus trip:

1. My band uniform.

2. My trombone.

3. My copy of Watership Down, which I'm supposed to finish by...yesterday. Oops.

None of these things help me block out the sub-populations of bus one: the low brass, the trumpets, and the band couples.

When I get on the bus, the first thing I do is look for Jonah, just because he's my friend's little brother, and I want to make sure he's okay. But when I see he's all settled in with two sophomore guys—Ben, who plays bari sax, and Jaden, who plays mellophone—I feel almost disappointed. Like, Jonah's only been in band for a week, and he already has people to sit with on the bus. What's wrong with me?

I end up taking the spot across the aisle from Brian, which turns out to be a front seat for the Saturday Night Hookup Extravaganza, starring Nicky Zukosky the sousaphone player and a tiny flute player named Malaika.

Before I can talk myself out of it, I lean across the aisle and say, "Hey, Brian, do you mind if I sit next to you?"

He passes me his trombone case, saying, "Put that next to yours, okay?" and then pats the empty space next to him.

"No switching seats while the bus is moving!" a band mom screeches the second I stand up, because having sex on the bus is fine but God forbid you stand up for a few seconds.

"Oooh, Meghan." Brian smirks at me.

I roll my eyes. "Whatever. I wanted to change my seat, that's all."

"Avoiding the band couples?"

"How did you guess?"

"I feel your pain," Brian says. "I feel your pain." Then he holds out his phone and offers me an earbud. "Here, this'll help," he says. "The Ultimate Trombone Playlist." He hits play: "Concerto for Trombone and Military Band," Christian Lindberg. "Sonata 'Vox Gabrieli,'" Joseph Alessi. "Popcorn Butter," Paul the Trombonist. "Piece for Two Tromboniums," J.J. Johnson and Kai Winding. "Track Suit," Minor Mishap Marching Band. "A Night in Tunisia," by Dizzy Gillespie and his band, including Melba Liston. Gram would be proud.

We pull up to Potomac High while Bonerama are rocking "Helter Skelter." Even with the earbuds in, Brian's kept up a steady stream of trombone talk the whole way here. He tells me he started taking lessons with this guy who's a high school band conductor out in the next county over, this guy who studied at the Oberlin Conservatory and then played in the Air Force jazz band and almost made it into the Baltimore Symphony a few years ago. Brian has to work at Target every spare minute he has to pay for lessons and gas, but he says it's totally worth it.

"If you want," he says, "I can give you his contact info. Maybe you could take lessons, too. I mean, no offense— you're fine for a newbie—but if you learned how to control your breathing—"

"Okay, everyone, attention please," Colleen says. She's managed to peel herself off Charlie long enough to remember she's the head drum major and more or less in charge of this whole thing. "We're gonna head inside in a few minutes. Get your uniforms on—that means your cummerbunds *and* your dickeys, *and* your flags, *and* your plumes. We're not gonna have another Carroll incident, right, guys?"

"RIGHT!" all the upperclassmen yell in unison.

"What happened at Carroll?" I ask Brian.

"Maya forgot her plume on the bus, so we lost, like, 10 points."

I know I'm supposed to be sympathetic, but since it was Maya, I have to laugh a little. Inside, anyway. Then I spend the next five minutes double-checking for my own plume.

"We'll have a little free time before the competition starts. Then we need everyone in the stands right at three o'clock. Douglass goes on first, then Fritchie, then us, then Carroll. Got it?"

"Got it," we all chorus, our voices muffled by jackets

and dickeys.

"Let's kick ass," Brian says to me. "And make sure you remember the D-flat in 'Signed, Sealed, Delivered.' I know we haven't played it much, but I keep forgetting to point that part out to you."

"Um. Sure," I say.

What D-flat?

#

My trombone playlist-induced good mood vanishes as soon as we step off the bus, when Kat spots me and fake-whispers to one of other the drummers, "Maybe this time all the newbies will be able to stay up on their feet."

But then I think about what Colleen said to me last week, after the football game. Kat's out of line. She's so out of line, she's not even in my section anymore. I can stop listening to her, and stop caring about what she   thinks. Like the girl in Labyrinth said, in the part that made me and Rachel cheer, she has no power over me.

So I do exactly what Colleen told me to do last week, and I say, "Stuff it, Kat."

Fine, so maybe it's not the most eloquent or mature way to tell someone off. Maybe my voice cracks a little on her name, and maybe I can't look her in the eye when I say it. But it works anyway. She blinks, and walks away. I know it's just for now, and she'll probably have plenty to say later, after the competition. But I also know I won't have to listen.

Next to me, Brian applauds. "Nicely done," he says. "But next time, I think you should tell her exactly where to stuff it. I have a list of suggestions in increasing order of discomfort." And I must be delirious, because I kind of want to hug him. Only for a second. But still.

Before I can, though, Charlie and Colleen catch up with us, with Jonah tagging along behind them. "Hey guys!" Charlie says, waving. He's pretty energetic, considering the workout he and Colleen were giving each other on the bus. "Colleen's gotta go fraternize with the enemy—"

"I have to say hi to the other drum majors, that's all," she says, rolling her eyes.

"But I'm gonna go grab us some seats so we don't miss the other bands."

"I'll see you guys later," says Colleen, kissing Charlie and then sprinting off in the direction of Carroll's fancy charter buses. I look back at our dingy yellow school buses, and I start feeling very, very outclassed.

That feeling sticks around for the whole competition, and I know I'm not alone in it. Douglass has their whole Harry Potter show on the field, complete with the dance line playing a Quidditch match. The Fritchie band does a show called "Metamorphosis," which is all classical pieces that Brian tells me are in the public domain. "That's how you get a classy-as-hell show for free—just grab a bunch of public-domain songs and give the whole thing a name that sounds deep. MABC judges fall for it every year." Fake-deep or not, they play pretty well through the songs, and it probably makes up for the fact that their marching isn't the strongest.

And then it's our turn, to march through what we've got of our show (we can march "My Girl" now, but we're standing in place during "Signed, Sealed, Delivered," and we haven't even touched "Reach Out I'll Be There" yet). We sound decent, and we look decent, but next to Douglass and Fritchie, we're a bunch of amateur losers. We leave the field to half-hearted applause, and I find myself wishing I had a tail to tuck between my legs. Maybe my flag would work.

The kids from Carroll cheer loudly as we march past them on our way off the field. For a second, I actually think, "Aw, isn't that nice, they're cheering for us, blah blah the spirit of friendly competition and good sportsmanship blah blah," and then I realize they're all being sarcastic. Some of them are doing fake slow claps, like the kind in movies, but most are chanting, "Motown TRAGIC! Motown TRAGIC!" And it's like, we didn't name our show. We're doing the best we can. But we can't say any of this, because we're marching, and we're at attention. And they should be, too, but their drum majors are yelling right along with everybody else.

As soon as we're past them, and Colleen calls, "Band! Horns down!" the flutes and trumpets start passing a message back through the rows. "We're boycotting Carroll's show," Dean says, leaning back to let the trombones know.

"No, we're not," Danny says.

"Why the hell not?"

"Because if we do, our girlfriends will kill us."

So that's settled. A few of the other trumpets, the ones who aren't going out with drum majors, do skip Carroll's show. Later we hear they never find the bus drivers, so they can't actually get on the buses, so they stand around in the parking lot like idiots. Which is no worse than standing around a football field looking like idiots, like we all did— but trombones are always happy for a chance to laugh at trumpets.

As mad as we are at Carroll, we all have to admit that their show rocks. It's James Bond-themed, with lots of tricky marching, and a low brass section that really does kick ass. Their show ends with a soloist from their school choir singing along to "Skyfall," and I swear she sounds just like Adele. Everyone else must think so, too, because the band gets a standing ovation.

There's no point in sticking around to hear the results, but MABC protocol is that all the bands have to stand on the field while the judges announce the scores. Carroll takes first, duh. Douglass takes second, Fritchie takes third, and we get…"A round of applause for all of our bands here tonight!" I wait for a giant hole to open up in the middle of the football field and swallow us up. It doesn't happen.

On the way home, the mood on the bus is somber. Funereal. Like we're the official marching band for some kind of funeral that people would hold late at night on a football field. People who don't have the money to hire a good marching band.

I sit next to Brian again. Charlie and Dean have joined us, too—their girlfriends have banished them to the front of the bus while they have an emergency drum major meeting—"either that or they want you guys out of the way so they can screw around with A.J.," Brian says, ducking before either of them can thwap him.

Then Brian stands up on top of the seat, and before any of the band boosters can tell him to sit down, he thrusts his arms up to the sky (or, rather, the ceiling of the bus) and starts singing "Bohemian Rhapsody," just like he promised. At an impossibly loud volume. And for someone who loves music so much, he really, really can't sing. So maybe we're all inspired, or maybe we all want to drown him out, but before long we've all joined in.

All around us, kids are singing along—kids who, five minutes ago, were sulking and snarking and cussing each other out. I look back at Jonah, who's belting along with his friends. When he catches my eye, he stops mid-"Galileo" and grins at me.

"A stupid-ass singalong cures all ills," Brian tells me. "Remember that."

"Got it," I say.

For once, Brian's probably right.

CHAPTER SEVEN

We host the next competition: the All-County Marching Band Expo. I know I should be excited that my parents and Ellie are finally going to see the show, but I'm dreading it all week, until Gram calls on Thursday night and asks to speak to me. Usually, she calls on Sundays, and usually, she starts with whoever answers the phone and we pass it around until she's talked to all of us. But as soon as I pick up, she says, "Well, sweetie, I've been sitting around all day thinking about you and your big show on Saturday, and I think I'm going to make the drive in for the weekend so I can see it. What do you think?"

"I think I better try not to fall down this time," I say, and she laughs, but it's true. If Gram's coming to see me march, it's going to be the best show I've done yet.

I find my parents in the living room, hold out the phone, and say, "Guess what? Gram's coming in for the competition!"

"She's doing what?" My mom grabs the phone from me and starts yelling into it. "Mom, are you crazy? You can't drive in all the way from—yes, I understand you want to—but why do you have to—and the traffic's going to be terrible—you could at least have given us a few days' notice!"

And here I thought this was good news.

As soon as Mom hangs up the phone, she starts freaking out about how her mother shouldn't be making the drive all by herself, and Dad freaks out back at her about how if she wants him to drive out to Ocean City and pick Gram up, she should ask him flat out. All of this is going on downstairs in the living room, but even back upstairs, with my door closed and Brian's Ultimate Trombone Playlist blaring, I can't drown it out all the way.

Gram arrives Saturday morning, just in time. I'm waiting by the window when she pulls into the driveway. When I run out to greet her, even though I'm taller than she is now, she still tries to sweep me up in a bear hug. "How's my trombone superstar?" she asks, kissing me on both cheeks.

"Terrified," I admit. Something about Gram always makes me tell the truth, even when I don't want to.

"You're going to be amazing out there this afternoon," she reassures me. "And I can't wait to hear you play 'My Girl.' You know your pop-pop used to sing that to me all the time."

I didn't know that. I wonder why not.

She grabs her suitcase out of the trunk and then hands me her Queen of Angels tote bag. "There's something special in here for you and Ellie," she says, but of course I already know what's inside: our favorite salt-water taffy. "And you thought you'd have to wait till you came out for

Thanksgiving!"

I give her another big hug, because even when her arms are full, Gram gives the best hugs. We head inside, and it's not too long before we're all squeezed into Dad's car and on our way to school.

It's almost like we've entered some parallel dimension where we're one of those perfect, together kind of families —except Mom and Dad are still sniping at each other, and Ellie's whining about how if she misses her soccer game, her coach is never gonna let her start again. At least Gram's happy, and she tries to keep a conversation going with me from the front passenger seat.

"Is your friend Rachel coming today?"

"Yeah, I told you, her brother's marching now, too, right?"

"Right, Jonah. The cute freshman."

"What?"

"Sweetie, I asked you last week if he was cute, and you didn't deny it. He sounds cute to me."

"God, Gram, he's only a freshman. And I never said he was cute," I protest, but I'm blushing and smiling, wondering what my face knows that I don't.

"Meghan's got a boyfriend," Ellie sing-songs automatically. It's not worth responding to her.

"I like both of them already," Gram declares. "Before I've even met them. I'm just that glad you're not spending time with that Dani girl anymore."

"What about Dani?" Mom asks. She and Dad have hit a

lull in their fight while he tries to find a parking spot.

"You know, I never liked her. She didn't have any personality. And she looked like a Shih Tzu."

"What?" I shriek, and then I can't stop giggling. Because it's so, so horrible. And it's so, so true.

"Mom!" says my mom. "What do you mean, Meghan's friend looks like a Shih Tzu?"

"I mean," Gram explains patiently, "that my friend Eileen at Queen of Angels has a Shih Tzu she carries around in her purse, and every time I see it, I want to call it Dani. Anyway," she says, before Mom can freak out any more, "how about that girl who was bothering you—the Tupperware girl? Is she going to be there?"

As soon as Gram mentions Kat, I realize that Kat hasn't yelled at me since the Carroll competition. Maybe telling her to stuff it actually worked.

"Who's been bothering you?" Mom asks.

"Where the hell am I supposed to put the car?" Dad's saying. "No one in this town has anything better to do today?"

"We're doing this for Meghan," Mom snaps, "and while you were complaining, you missed two spots."

Mom's already forgotten about her question, but Gram hasn't. "You point that Kat girl out to me, and I'll keep my eye on her. 'Tupperware.'" She says it the way someone else might say "kitten strangler," and I love her for it.

We finally park the car, and Gram's "Good luck!" follows me as I enter the band room.

I join the other trombones and start unpacking my case just as Brian asks, between mouthpiece buzzes, "You guys going to the dance tonight?"

Charlie puts a few drops of oil on the ends of his slide. "Yeah, we're doubling with Kenzie and Dean. How 'bout you?"

"Solo. Aka 'available for the taking by any eligible hot chicks.'" Brian waggles his eyebrows. I almost feel embarrassed for him.

"What about you, Meghan?" Charlie asks, leaning over to me. "What?" My mouthpiece is caught in the chain on my jacket, and untangling it is taking up more brain power than it should.

"Are you going to the dance?"

I barely even knew there was a dance happening, and I can't think of anything I'd want to do less after a day at a band competition. "Should I?"

Charlie shrugs. "Everybody does. I figured you'd be going with some other newbies or something."

In spite of myself, I look over at the clarinets. Dani's showing off what looks like a fresh manicure, and they're all squealing. I haven't talked to Dani in over a week. And when I've been hanging out with Rachel, or goofing around with the other trombones, I've been able to convince myself it doesn't matter: she was never a good friend, and I have better friends now, and anyway, Gram's totally right about her looking like a Shih Tzu.

"I guess not," I say.

"Oh, come on, you've gotta go to the dance," Brian says, because Brian refuses to drop things, and I should know that by now.

I'm not the kind of girl who goes to dances. I'm more the kind of girl who makes big Saturday night plans with fuzzy pajamas, Netflix, and hot chocolate. Which is exactly what I had on the schedule for tonight.

"Meghannnn, you should cooooome" Brian pleads, batting his eyelashes at me, and it's strangely adorable. I never noticed before, but his eyes are the exact color of blueberries.

"Fine," I say, because Mr. Coffman's about to call us to attention, and there's no way I can win this argument, and also, why the hell not?

"I'd go, but I'm bowling with Ben and Jaden tonight," Jonah says, even though nobody's asked him.

"If you survive the pyramid," Brian mutters.

"Oh, God," Jonah groans, slumping down in his seat. "The pyramid."

The pyramid is what you might call the bane of Jonah's existence. In the last week, we've finally gotten "Signed, Sealed, Delivered" on the field, and at the end of the song, the whole band is supposed to form this giant pyramid, and the person at the top of the pyramid was supposed to be Kat. Which means, of course, that now, it's Jonah. And somehow, poor Jonah, the newest of the newbies, is supposed to move backwards, without looking behind him, into the exact point of this pyramid we're all creating—this pyramid *he can't see.*

And, okay, if you know what you're doing, it shouldn't be too hard: he's right up front on the 50-yard line, and all he has to do is move back ten steps. But he keeps obsessing over just what a "step" is. Like, for example, his feet are bigger than mine, and a little bigger than Charlie's, but smaller than Brian's—so when the drum majors or Mr. Coffman talk about "steps," Jonah can't get it into his head that he needs to take ten steps—I mean, literally, step backwards ten times. He keeps going, "Ten me steps? Ten Brian steps? Ten Meghan steps?" And then he'll look around and catch sight of someone like Malaika the piccolo player, and say, "I hope you don't mean, like, ten Malaika-sized steps, because I don't think I can manage that." (And then Malaika will get this close to jamming her piccolo up his ass, but so far the other flutes have managed to restrain her.)

According to Rachel, he'd been freaking out about the pyramid every night at home, too—and measuring his feet and everybody else's, which had made things even more annoying. At lunch the other day, she even asked me if I could do something about it. "He'll listen to you," she said. "You're, like, his trombone queen."

"I think Jonah is just gonna be Jonah," I told her. "You're his sister. You should know that by now."

"I know, I know," she sighed. "I know he's being Jonah. I just keep kind of hoping he'll *stop.*"

In the present, Jonah's fallen into a pit of despair. "I

don't even remember why I joined marching band. It was your fault, right, Meghan? You brainwashed me, and any minute now, I'm gonna come to my senses and drop this class for something easier, like AP Calc, right?"

I think back to falling down at the first football game. "It gets better," I reassure Jonah, with all the authority of someone who's been in marching band one whole month longer than he has. "First, stop listening to Brian—"

"Hey!"

"And stop worrying so much. I bet you kick that pyramid's ass today." I hold up my hand for a high-five.

He gives it a squeeze instead.

I never noticed this before, but his eyes are the exact color of Hershey's kisses.

I really shouldn't have skipped breakfast.

#

Maybe it's my fault for not totally believing it when I say it, but Jonah? Does not kick the pyramid's ass. In fact, the pyramid kicks his ass. He completely screws it up, somehow managing to take about 20 steps to the side instead of 10 straight back, and he collides with Dani and almost takes the whole clarinet section down with him. And so at least half the band's convinced Jonah has humiliated them so badly that their high school careers, and probably their adult lives, are ruined.

While Fritchie plays through their weird

"Metamorphosis" show, Charlie calls a trombone meeting over concession-stand junk food.

"So, Jonah," he says, going into Section Leader mode. "The number one thing you need to know about marching band is, everyone screws up. Especially at their first game."

"Tell me one person who screwed up as bad as I did," Jonah challenges him.

Charlie thinks. "Did you see Brian during that last horns up?"

"No."

"Well, he was like a half-second late."

"I was not!" Brian pipes up.

"That. Is not. The same. At all."

"I know!" I volunteer. "Dani almost tripped."

"Because I bumped into her," Jonah reminds me.

Oh, yeah.

Charlie glances at me. "Meghan, what about your first football game? Before Jonah joined?"

Way to ruin my one-whole-month-before-Jonah seniority, Charlie.

"What happened?" Jonah wants to know.

"Nothing happened."

"Meghan, tell him."

"I played a D-flat instead of a D-natural," I say.

"You *fell down*," Charlie corrects me.

"Oh, yeah," I say, like it slipped my mind.

"So I'm really not the only one," Jonah says, and he looks so relieved, it's almost worth it.

Charlie checks his phone. "Okay, guys, see you back in the stands in a few." He bounds off towards the bleachers, probably to meet Colleen.

"I'm gonna get some more food," Brian says, finishing off the last of his nachos. "How about you guys?"

"I think I'll just head back to the stands," Jonah says, and I find myself agreeing with him.

The two of us walk together along the bleachers, and pass my parents, Gram, and Ellie sitting in the fifth row of the bleachers, right in front of the 50-yard line. Gram's cheering for me and waving a pom-pom she must have bought at the school boosters' table. I wave back.

"Is that your family?" Jonah asks.

I nod. "My older sister's at college. But that's my parents, my baby sister, and my grandma. She came in from Ocean City just for the show."

I'm not sure why I'm telling Jonah all this, and I'm worried I'm probably boring him, but he smiles and says, "That's really cool." Then he waves back to them and calls, "Hi, Meghan's family!"

Gram mouths to me, "Jonah?" and when I nod, she gives me a thumbs-up. Oh, my God.

I'm praying Jonah didn't notice any of that, and then I'm saved by Rachel, who runs down the bleacher steps to meet us. "You guys sounded great," she says.

"Sounded, maybe," Jonah grumbles.

I've got to change the subject before Jonah goes all despair-pit-y again. "Hey, we should go to that dance thing tonight," I blurt out.

"Are you on drugs?" Rachel asks.

"Come on, it'll be fun," I say. "Or at least, it'll be so bad it's entertaining." I warm to my own sales pitch. "And maybe some couple will break up in the middle of the Chicken Dance or something."

"Okay, if I missed something like that, I'd kill myself," she says. "I'll see if my mom can give us a ride. And if I can find something to wear."

"If I can still get into the dress from my cousin's wedding last year, anything's possible."

"Dude, you're getting me to go to a dance. Obviously, anything's possible."

Rachel waves on her way back to her seat, and Jonah and I walk back to the band section, where we've left our trombones.

"Thanks for earlier, by the way," he says as we sit down on the cold bleachers again. He says it mostly to his trombone, and to the flip folder that's somehow gotten caught on his spit key, but I know what he means.

#

At dinner, everybody in my family has something nice to say about the show ("Who bumped into the clarinets?" Ellie asks). Then, I announce that I'm going to the dance and Mrs. Reznik is picking me up in an hour. Mom and Dad look surprised and relieved, the way they always do when it looks like I have something resembling a social life. Ellie can't understand how I could go to a dance without a date, but that's fifth graders for you. And Gram says, "Good for you, sweetie. Have a wonderful time."

I take a quick shower, squeeze into the dress (it's a bit too small, but not so bad anyone will notice), fight a losing battle with my frizzy hair, and add a little lip gloss and mascara. I only poke myself in the eye once.

When I come downstairs, Gram's waiting for me. "Let me see," she says, and I twirl around like when I was a little girl showing off my new Christmas dress for her.

"You look beautiful. But I think it needs something." And she hands me a little claddagh necklace, with the tiniest diamond in the center. Her birthstone. My birthstone, too.

"Your pop-pop gave this to me, a long time ago. I wasn't too much older than you then. I was going to give it to you when you turned sixteen, but…I think tonight's the perfect night for it." She fastens it in the back for me. "I can't believe how grown-up you look, Meghan," Gram says, and she gives me a hug. Even here, she smells like the ocean.

The Rezniks' SUV pulls up in our driveway. Gram, Mom, and Dad kiss me goodbye, and I'm off.

Mrs. Reznik's driving, Rachel's in the front seat, and next to me in the middle is Jonah, who makes a squinchy face at me and says, "Hey, Meghan. You look weird."

"Jonah!" his mom and sister chorus from the front, while I check to see if I've grown a third eye or a horn or anything.

"I just meant she looks different, that's all. Not in a bad way."

"Then you could give her a compliment, Jonah," Mrs. Reznik says. "You could say, 'You look nice, Meghan.'"

"You look nice, Meghan," Jonah parrots.

"'You look like a beautiful princess, Meghan,'" Rachel suggests.

He looks out the window and slumps in his seat. "Shut up, Rachel."

"Mom! Jonah told me to shut up."

"Honey, I think you deserved it," Mrs. Reznik says, as she lets us off at the gym entrance. "See you here at 11, girls."

I'm about to close the door, when Jonah says one more time, "You look nice, Meghan."

"So do you," I say automatically, because that's what you do with girls, but of course, Jonah's not a girl.

Mrs. Reznik pulls away before I can put any more of my body parts in my mouth, but Rachel's still there, and she's making the same squinchy face her brother just made at me. "What the hell?" she asks.

I shrug, and we walk inside the gym.

Entering the gym is almost—but not quite—like the time I stepped into the bleacher underworld at the first football game. No one's doing anything too illicit, at least not that I can see, but everyone looks different. Everyone looks like grownups. The guys have all traded in their T-shirts and jeans for jackets and ties, and even the other soap and water girls are glammed up in black dresses, makeup, and fancy updos. Then there's me, in a year-old dress that barely fits, and Rachel, in a thrift-store dress she picked up on her way home from the football game. I start wondering if she and I will get kicked out for being underdressed, or under-coiffed, or something.

The gym itself doesn't look too impressive. The lights are all off except for a few spotlights in the corners, there's some blue balloons and gold crepe paper hung randomly around the room, and there's a big painted banner on one of the walls that says, "A NIGHT TO REMEMBER." Meanwhile, the DJ is playing a song about butts. I can't remember what it's called, but man, do I remember how much it sucks.

"I hate this song," I shout over the thumping bass.

"All right-thinking people hate this song," Rachel yells back.

We stand next to each other awkwardly, watching the rest of the school dance and sing about how great their butts are. Dani and Maya are in the middle of a group of clarinets and drummers, and they're doing some stupid dance together, like they've choreographed it. Knowing Dani, they probably have.

"You know," Rachel says, outside my head. "We're kind of in the middle of the dance floor. And if we stand here any longer, they might make us start dancing."

"Good point," I say. I scan the gym for a quiet place to

stand, or maybe a place to hide. Any place I won't be able to see Dani. Instead, I catch sight of Charlie, who grins and waves us over to where he's standing, in a big clump with Colleen and a bunch of other seniors.

"Meghan!" Charlie greets me. "You made it!"

"You and Brian inspired me," I tell him.

"What?"

"You! And Brian! Inspired me!"

"What?"

I give up. "This is Jonah's sister, Rachel," I say, because she's way better at projecting her voice than I am, and she likes talking more than I do.

I tune out of the conversation and watch Charlie and Colleen together. He's standing behind her, with his arms around her waist, and every once in a while he whispers something to her that makes her turn around and kiss him. For the first time, I wonder what's going to happen to them when they go to college next fall. It's probably not going to be like one of those TV shows where the couple and all their friends end up at the same school together, right in their hometown.

A slow song comes on, and Colleen drags Charlie onto the dance floor. The remaining seniors stare at me and Rachel for a minute, then turn away.

"This kind of sucks," I say.

"No kidding," says Rachel.

We wander around the gym for a while longer, saying hi to kids who are at our level of uncool. At one point, Rachel finds some girls she knows from art club, and they're all almost as good at talking loud as she is. So they all start yelling at each other about pottery or something, and I stand there feeling dumb and lonely and wondering if it's ever going to be 11. The DJ switches to another slow song, one that was big when I was in sixth grade or so, and I try to remember what movie it was from. Something with a lot of explosions, and maybe the world ended and everybody died. Lucky them.

Then there's a tap on my shoulder. I turn around, half-expecting the Under-Coiffed Police. Actually, it's Brian.

"Hey," I say. He's actually looking semi-decent. Like all the other guys, he's in a suit and tie, and even though the suit jacket looks a little too small, and the tie is decorated with a sheet music pattern, he's almost...well...cute.

"Meghan!" he exclaims, smiling at me. "Dude, I'm so glad you made it!" He glances at my outfit, his eyes resting a little too long on my boobs. Ew. "You look...different."

"Different" again. What the hell does that mean, anyway?

"Um," I say intelligently. I want to be mad at Brian—it's kind of his fault I'm here, after all—but before I can be, he blurts out, "Hey, Meghan, listen—uh—wanna dance?"

At first I don't think I heard him right. "Huh?"

He looks hurt, and I realize I did hear him right, and now he thinks I'm trying to reject him. And somehow, from somewhere, maybe from the same place that's convinced me almost every week this fall that I can stand in front of hundreds of people and play whole notes on my trombone, I get the confidence to hold out my hand. And now he's putting his arms around my waist, and I'm putting my arms around his waist, and then looking around and seeing that all the other girls have their arms around the guys' necks, and I try to move mine up and they get all tangled in his, and then oh, my God, Brian's kissing me.

Wait, what?

It's so fast when he kisses me—just a brush of his lips across mine—that at first I think either I imagined it, or he bumped into me by accident while I was trying to get my arms where they were supposed to be. But then, once our arms are all in the right place, he does it again. And it's still kind of a peck, and I still don't have the chance to figure out what I'm supposed to be doing back, with my lips or my hands or anything, really. My brain barely even has time to register that I've been kissed—that I just got my first kiss, and my second kiss, from Brian, during the song from the movie where everybody died and the world ended. And then he says, "You're, like, a great friend, Meghan," and he won't even look at me, but he keeps his hands on my waist, and when the song is over, he gives me an awkward hug and takes off for the gym doors, mumbling something about having to pee.

#

The next morning, I wake up early and lie in bed

replaying yesterday in my head like a movie. Playing in front of my whole family at the halftime show. Gram giving me her necklace. Going to the dance with Rachel. Getting my first kiss, *finally*. From *Brian*. Later, trying to tell Rachel what had happened, and having to mime it, because the music was so loud, and her still not getting it, and going, "Brian BIT YOU?" Spending the whole car ride home making vampire jokes with Rachel, and giggling helplessly until her mom finally threatened to kick us out and make us walk.

Then I remember what Rachel had said at our sleepover, about making that list, and I tear out a sheet of paper from my French notebook and get started.

Reasons I Like Marching Band:

1. Band camp. As hard as it sucked this year. Because even though no one ever likes to admit it, summer vacation gets old by August, and band camp gives you something to do and a good reason to get out of your house. And because next year? I'm not gonna be a newbie anymore.

2. Football games. Because for some reason, spending Friday nights at school, with athletes and cheerleaders, and playing the Notre Dame Victory March until you puke is... kind of fun.

3. Competitions. See #2. Making noise on the bus rides.

Getting out on the field and trying to put on a great show. Staring in amazement at the other bands (even Carroll). And that moment when we stand at attention and wait for our scores—that moment of anticipation, that this time, something good might happen. (Sure, it never does. But for a minute, we can almost believe it will.)

4. The way the drums echo off the stands. The greasy, sweaty football stadium smell. The sound of so many people playing the same song, chanting the same cheers, doing the same thing. Together.

5. One more, and it's maybe the most important: Because sometimes things happen that you never would have expected—things that are pretty cool—and you know they never would've happened if you hadn't been in marching band in the first place.

HORNS UP

CHAPTER ONE

Nina comes home right before Columbus Day weekend, which we're supposed to spend in Ocean City with Gram, when for once I don't have a game or a competition to worry about. But on Thursday, the day after Nina arrives, Mom wakes us all up before dawn, pounding on our bedroom doors and saying, "Girls, get packed, we have to go now."

"Where?" I mumble, still half asleep.

"To Gram's," she says.

It turns out that if it's early enough in the morning, you can get your daughters to do anything you want them to do without asking you why. Across the hall, Nina starts banging her dresser drawers open and shut. Ellie sleepwalks into the bathroom. I stare at my suitcase, which is barely visible under a pile of clothes I should have hung up days ago, and then get up and get started.

Mom and Dad are in their room with the door closed,

and they've turned up the TV news so we can't hear them fighting. I peek into Nina's room.

"What?" She's sitting on her bed, completely dressed, with her packed suitcase next to her. Sometimes I really wonder if she's human.

"What's going on?"

She sighs. "I have no idea."

Ellie sidles up behind me, with her toothbrush still poking out of her mouth. "Why are we going on vacation early?"

"I don't know," I say.

And Nina says, "I don't think it's vacation."

"Girls." Dad's in the hall with us now, too. His eyes are red. "You'd better come downstairs with me."

We follow Dad down to the kitchen, and he sits us down at the kitchen table. "Girls, it's your grandmother." His voice sounds weird, and I realize it's because he's trying not to cry in front of us.

I want to ask what's going on, but something holds me back. Because as long as I don't know, it doesn't have to be real.

But Dad keeps talking. "She went into the hospital a few days ago with stomach pains. It's...it's pancreatic cancer."

It's just words, and I don't even know exactly what they mean, but it still feels like someone's rammed me in the stomach with the business end of a sousaphone. A tiny voice in my brain starts chanting, "No no no no no," and it's not until I catch Ellie looking at me that I realize I'm saying it out loud. And even then, I can't stop.

"It's *what?*" Nina demands. "When did you find out? How come you didn't tell us?"

"What's pancreatic?" asks Ellie.

"Your mother didn't tell you? I told her we had to tell you as soon as we found out." Dad storms out of the kitchen and back up the stairs. The yelling starts again, before they can close the bedroom door this time. Mom says she just wanted Nina to have one last happy family vacation. Dad says she can't make things go away by not dealing with them. Then the door finally slams.

"What's pancreatic?" Ellie repeats, like she can't hear them.

"Pancreatic cancer," Nina says flatly. "It means she's probably not gonna get better."

I stare at the pattern on the kitchen tablecloth. Red square, white square, blue square, white square. Red square, white square, blue square, white square. No, no, no, no, no.

Mom stomps down the stairs. "Get your things. We have to get on the road."

#

It's a weird, terrible, long, long weekend.

I've never been in Gram's house without her. It feels wrong. It feels worse knowing we're all here, in her house, while she's lying in a bed in some hospital.

My parents fight the whole way to Ocean City. Dad

thinks we need to see Gram and spend as much time with her as we can while we can, so he wants us at the hospital with them every single day. Mom thinks it's going to upset us too much to see Gram the way she is. Neither of them asks us what we think. They're not really talking to us at all.

Mom wins the argument this time. She and Dad spend Thursday and Friday at the hospital, and Nina, Ellie, and I sit around Gram's house by ourselves, eating frozen Girl Scout cookies and canned pineapple when we get hungry. We keep the TV on for company, and we turn it up loud, as Ellie switches back and forth between ESPN and the Disney Channel.

Rachel and Jonah both message me on Thursday afternoon, in the group text we've kept going since the night of the sleepover, wondering where I am. ("I thought OC trip was tomorrow??" Jonah types. "Brian keeps yelling at me about sforzandos. COME BACK.")

I'm hoping a reply of "family crap" will be enough, because talking about it any more will make it realer than it already is, but they both text back with so many different kinds of sad stickers, I kind of feel I owe them something better. I let them know Gram's sick, and Jonah sends back a sticker of a bear holding a heart-shaped balloon. I keep my phone off for most of the next few days, but every once in a while, I turn it on just to look at that little bear.

When I can't take the living room noise anymore, I shut myself up in Gram's bedroom, in the overstuffed chair next to the window, holding the rosary beads she keeps on her night table, next to the picture of her and Pop-Pop on their wedding day. I don't know how to pray the rosary, but I know she does it, and holding the beads feels like holding her hand, like any second now she's going to come in the room and sit down with me, and we'll start talking about band, and Rachel and Jonah, and her friends at Queen of Angels and the senior center. She'll tell me about the new book she got out from the library—one of those soapy Irish novels where all the characters are all in love with the wrong people—and then she'll ask me what I want for dinner, and what I want to see most when we go to the boardwalk tomorrow. And I'll have to think about it for a minute, because no one ever asks me those things but her.

And when I remember Gram isn't here, when I remember why we're really here, I start crying the way no one but Gram has ever seen me cry.

I know when Mom and Dad talk about me with their friends—I know they do it; all parents do—they say I'm the steady one, I'm the low-maintenance one. Nina's high-strung, Nina's got a temper. Ellie's a bundle of energy, Ellie's still a baby. Meghan's the middle child. Meghan's the easy one. I want it to be true, because otherwise I don't know who I am for them. But it's not true. I'm a mess. And I want my Gram. Now.

I don't know what to do about it, though. It's Nina who figures it out.

For most of Thursday and Friday, Nina doesn't say a word. She sits in Gram's chair, with a book lying closed on her lap, staring at the photos on the living room walls. Gram and Pop-Pop outside the Majestic Theatre in New York. Mom and Dad's wedding at Queen of Angels. All of us at the beach, back when Ellie was barely even walking. Baby me with spaghetti all over my face. Gram and her senior center friends in Ireland two summers ago. She was supposed to go again this summer.

Finally, on Friday afternoon, Nina turns off the TV and says, "I hate this family."

I stare at her. Ellie keeps one eye on the TV in case the game reappears inside it. "

What kind of people think they can keep something like this from their kids?"

We don't answer. We can't answer.

"I mean, seriously. They must have known she was sick for days. And they didn't say a word until they couldn't put it off any longer? And we're not even allowed to see her? We're supposed to sit here in her house and pretend everything's fine? I don't think so." She grabs her messenger bag and stomps out the door.

Ellie and I look at each other, then at Gram's empty chair. I grab the remote and turn the TV back on, and we sit frozen in our seats until late that night, when Mom and Dad come home with Nina, and the three of them go to bed without a word.

Saturday morning, Nina wakes me up. "Get up and get dressed," she says, looming over the couch bed Ellie and I are sharing. "We're going to the hospital today. I walked there last night and told Mom and Dad they had to let us."

"What?" First I think it's a dream. I can't make her words make sense in my head.

"Well, say 'thank you,'" she tells me.

"What?"

She shakes her head, and then holds out her hand and pulls me up into her arms. I don't remember the last time we hugged. It feels weird, but safe. Like we're stuck in something terrible, but at least we're stuck in it together.

She pulls away, and I know the tears in her eyes match the tears in mine. "Come on, let's wake up Ellie."

We eat granola bars for breakfast, all five of us standing up in the kitchen, and no one says a word until Dad grabs the keys and says, "Let's go."

I've only been in a hospital twice before—once when Ellie fell off her bike and got a concussion, and once when she broke her elbow in the middle of a soccer game. The hospital here is bigger than the hospital back home, and on the floor where Gram is staying, instead of kids with cute sports injuries, it's old people moaning and grunting, and people with oxygen masks being pushed through the hallways, and weird beeping sounds. "Mom," Dad says as we crowd into the room (our own mom isn't talking; she's wearing her sunglasses, and her lips are drawn in a thin pale line), "look who we brought."

Gram raises her head from her pillow a bit, and gives us a tiny smile. Her dyed light brown hair is fading to its natural gray and white, and it looks like it hasn't been combed in a few days. Her eyes are glassy, and even though it's only been two weeks since I last saw her, she looks like she's lost about 30 pounds. Her cheeks are sunken, her skin is jaundiced, and her collar bones jut out like they could cut you if you hugged her. I'm afraid to hug her. I'm afraid I'll break her.

Nina rushes toward the bed and gives Gram a huge hug. Ellie stands back, staring at her sneakers and twisting a strand of hair around her right pinky finger. I take a few steps forward, holding my breath. Then the beeping noises get louder, until I can't hear anything else, and my head starts pounding along with the beeps, and my knees buckle. The world gets hot and white, and I feel the vomit rise up to the back of my mouth, and I run for the nearest bathroom, where I lose my breakfast and some remnants of last night's attempt at dinner as well.

Mom drives me back to Gram's.

For the rest of Saturday and Sunday, I'm stuck on the couch flipping through the channels and sipping flat ginger ale. I know I'm not really sick—it was a reaction to being in the hospital, or something—but it's like Mom is relieved to have any excuse to keep one of us away. I watch TV with the volume loud enough to shake the pictures on the walls, I watch ancient sitcoms until their laugh tracks drown out every worry in my head, and I watch the sun set earlier each night until the doctors say Gram is stable enough for now. She can go home, and so can we.

CHAPTER TWO

Home is weird when we get back. Mom and Dad fight even more, about hospice care and insurance costs and how to make sure Gram's being taken care of when we're three hours away from her. Then they turn around and yell at me and Ellie—random, disconnected things. Ellie leaves her soccer cleats in the living room, and Dad says, "Dammit, Ellie, we don't have a maid, and you're not a baby anymore. It's about time you start acting your age." I come home a little late from Rachel and Jonah's house, and Mom says, "Dammit, Meghan, if you don't stop slacking off with your friends, you're never gonna get a college scholarship." Ellie says, "God, Dad, I forgot, okay?" I say, "God, Mom, I'm only 10 minutes late." I don't know about anyone else, but all I'm really saying is, "I'm scared."

Every time the phone rings, everybody freezes, expecting the hospice nurse with bad news, even though it's usually robo-calls, or sometimes Mom's younger brother, Uncle Eddie, who lives in Ohio and can't get time off work to come out here.

I'm getting good at pushing thoughts to the back of my mind when I don't want to deal with them. I've discovered that the less time I spend at the house, the easier it is not to worry about Gram—or to get in the way of Mom and Dad, who use all of their energy either arguing with each other or looking for either me or Ellie to dump all of their stress on. So I fill all of my time with other stuff:

1. First, marching band, of course. Every day in school, every Tuesday and Thursday night, and most Fridays and Saturdays, too. The more I march, the louder I play, and the goofier the other trombones and I are together, the less room I have in my head for the bad thoughts.

2. Obsessing, briefly, over Brian and what the kisses at the dance meant. Maybe for another girl, they would have led to nerdy trombone love, holding hands during Paul the Trombonist livestreams and making out to Sousa marches or something. But what happens instead is, well, nothing. By the time I get back from Gram's, it's like he and I never kissed at all. I spend a whole lunch period analyzing it with Rachel, who may be even more clueless about guys than I am ("But you live with one," I say. "He's not a guy," she explains. "He's a little brother."). Then I go through the advice columns in my sisters' magazine collections. Nina's magazines tell me to smash the patriarchy. Ellie's tell me to switch lipsticks. Again. No. Help. At. All.

Eventually, I let it go. I mean, I was, like, a good friend. Right?

Brian does give me his trombone teacher's email address —"Get in touch with him and set up some lessons. You're gonna rock so hard once you've got better breath control."

First, I think that's a weird dig at my kissing skills, but then I remember that the kisses were so quick they didn't require any breath control, or any skill or effort on my part. So, I started taking lessons with Mr. Martin, who lets his students call him Chip, even though, according to his business cards, his first name is Anthony.

The lessons are hard work, but I end up loving them. When I babysit for the kids across the street, I put all the money I make toward buying the Arban book, which Chip and Brian call the trombone bible, and I spend more time at home practicing than I ever did before. And when Brian tells me he's auditioning for All-State Band, and he says, "Meghan, you have to try out, too," it almost feels like something I can do.

3. Hanging out at Rachel and Jonah's. As much as possible. They live close enough that I can ride my bike over, but their house always feels like it's in a different world. A world where families are normal, like on TV.

Sometimes when I'm over there, it's me and Rachel hanging out, gossiping or doing homework or planning our next stop-motion extravaganza. Sometimes, there's a group of us—like Rachel's art club friends Ilana and Claire, or Jonah's band friends, Ben and Jaden.

Most of the time, though, it's me, Rachel, and Jonah. And most of the time, that's fine. Except when Rachel gets kind of pissy, because Jonah and I are talking too much about marching band, or because we're supposed to be having an Othello tournament but it's ended up being me and Jonah facing off against each other for an hour while she sits around and reads for English class. But she's probably annoyed because she's not in marching band. And because she sucks at Othello.

When Rachel starts working on a film about Hanukkah, she asks me and Jonah to put something together for a soundtrack. Well, what she actually says is, "You guys are so obsessed with your damn trombones, I might as well profit from it," and then she stomps up the basement stairs and leaves us alone.

It shouldn't be weird to be alone with Jonah. I spend half of my time sitting next to him or marching next to him in band, and the rest of my time hanging out with him at his house. But we've never really been alone together before. And Rachel's footsteps are still echoing in the room, even though the basement stairs are carpeted.

"Do you know any Hanukkah songs?" I ask. Does my voice always sound that stupid?

"Do I?" Jonah says, and he starts singing loudly, to the tune of "My Darling Clementine": "Spin the dreidel, spin the dreidel, spin the dreeeeiiiiiidel, everyone!"

"Um—"

"I know songs for other holidays, too," he continues. "Dip the apples in the honey, Rosh Hashaaaaaanah time is here—"

"All Jewish songs are to the tune of 'Clementine'?"

"Yes," he says solemnly. "My people have a very proud

musical tradition. We just didn't learn anything about it growing up."

"So we'll play a duet of 'Clementine'? And Rachel will be good with that?"

"Yeah, sure, bring your trombone next time you come over."

So I do, the next day, and Jonah and I end up hanging out together for most of the afternoon. He's put together a minor-key, up-tempo version of "Clementine" that Rachel deemed "just klezmer enough." ("You guys know there are, like, actual Hanukkah songs," she says, but Jonah feigns complete innocence.) We play through that a few times, and then we end up running through the music for the band show, and some of the stuff we play in the stands. And it turns out, Jonah can really play. I tell him he should think about taking lessons with Chip, maybe in the spring, when marching band is over.

When Chip decides I should start learning jazz, he gives me a book of "easy jazz duets" and says maybe Brian and I could get together sometime and play through them. But I know exactly who I want to practice these songs with, and it's not Brian. After my lesson, I text Jonah to see about coming over, and he replies immediately, "YES. PLEASE." So I get Dad to drive me straight from my lesson to Jonah's house. Jonah and Rachel's house.

Rachel opens the door. "Meghan! Dude! I was just about to text you."

"Actually," I say, "I'm here to see Jonah."

Rachel's face falls, but she doesn't say another word as she lets me in.

She doesn't have to say anything. I didn't spend months chasing after Dani without learning what it means to be a shitty friend. And I know I'd be pissed if Rachel showed up at my house and said she wanted to hang out with Ellie. But that would never happen. Rachel and Ellie aren't friends. They don't have anything in common. Jonah and I…we might even have more in common than Rachel and I do, if I'm honest with myself. But then, like I said, I'm getting really good at not being honest with myself.

"I'm sorry," I say, and I mean it. "I've got this book to show him…We'll talk later, okay?"

"Fine," she says, stomping upstairs without looking back at me. I want to follow her and try to fix this. But more than that, more than I want to let myself know, I want to see Jonah. So I head for the basement, where I know he'll be waiting.

#

The next Friday, Carroll comes to town to crush us at football and marching at the same time. The day of the game, Mr. Coffman and the drum majors spend the whole period giving us pep talks about how much we've grown over the last few months, and how fantastic our show is, and how our goal is to entertain the audience, and how if they start yelling, "Motown TRAGIC!" at us, we should just use it as fuel to make our show EVEN BETTER. It is, as Brian mutters under his breath, complete bullshit.

We're all tense all day. Jonah tells me he almost didn't come to school today, because he's so freaked about the stupid pyramid. So he and I stay after school until the game, and we go over to the field and practice. After half an hour or so of marching with an imaginary band behind us, Jonah is finally seeming a little calmer, and he says, "Hey, Meghan, I was gonna go bowling with Ben and Jaden before the game, and maybe get dinner there. You should come, too." I say yes.

I wouldn't say I hate bowling—it's more like I'm not a fan of stuff I suck at, and bowling falls in that category. We had a bowling unit once, in eighth grade gym class, where we'd walk over to Dulaney Lanes and do duckpin bowling. It was cool that we got to leave school during the school day (even if it was only for half an hour, and with our gym teachers), but otherwise, it was just another excuse for all the coordinated kids to yell at me. I haven't bowled since then. But I'm not going home if I can help it, even for the hour or two I have to kill before we have to be back in the band room. And spending time with Jonah is always fun. So we meet up with Ben and Jaden and walk over to Dulaney Lanes together.

Jonah turns out to be a decent bowler—not just the kind of bowler who actually knocks pins down (which is impressive enough to me), but the kind who gets spares and strikes, and brings his own ball and shoes. It's nice seeing Jonah feeling confident about something, seeing him smile that big goofy smile when he gets a strike, watching him get all bashful when we cheer for him. It's like when we're hanging out at his house and kicking each other's asses at Othello, or rocking our jazz duets together, except here we're in the real world, so everybody else gets to see how cool he is, too.

Of course, it's not really about the game. It's about eating junk and acting stupid. And as good as I am at both of those things, Jonah and his friends are even better.

It starts because Jonah's earwormed with this stupid *Looney Tunes* song, from the one with the frog in the top hat, and he takes to singing the song and doing the little dance every time he gets a strike.

I think it's adorable, not that I'd say that out loud. By the third performance, though, Ben's had enough, and he says, "Whatever, man, anything released in the twenty-first century is better than *Looney Tunes*."

"Ooh, them's fightin' words," Jaden says. But it's true, as anyone who knows Jonah should know.

Jonah turns around to face Ben, bowling ball in hand. "I'm gonna let this go. Just this once. Because I know you're just jealous that I'm winning."

"I'm not jealous. I just hate that stupid frog."

"Do not talk about Michigan J. Frog that way," Jonah says, and he whirls back around, bowls another strike, and starts to sing again. Then Ben starts singing, too—an old *Family Guy* song.

I look over at Jaden. "So how long is this gonna go on?"

"Hard to say. Usually I'm the tiebreaker."

"Well, Jonah's song has choreography…but Ben's has fart jokes. So it's a tough call."

"Finally, someone who understands," he says, and I think he's serious.

The guys' energy must be catching or something, because on my turn, I discover that if I wave my hands around enough, and if I yell, "GO! GO! GO! OVER THERE!" enough, I can sometimes get the ball to stay out of the gutter. Jonah says maybe I'd do even better if I didn't touch the ball at all, and moved it with my mind instead. I figure it's worth a try. Which makes my next turn very long, because as it turns out, I do not have the Force.

Ben grumbles, "All the wrong people think they're Jedis," and Jaden points out that we have to be back at school in half an hour.

"All right," says Jonah. "For the rest of the game, we're doing speed bowling."

"Speed bowling! Hell yeah!" Ben bellows.

"God help us all," says Jaden.

"What's speed bowling?" I ask, regretting the words as soon as I've said them.

"I will demonstrate," Jonah says with great dignity, and then he sprints to the lane, grabs the first ball he can, hurls it down the lane with a thud, and runs back to us, arms flailing.

All ten pins come crashing down. Unbelievable.

"The important thing," he says, panting a little, "is to get out of the way of the PHYSICS!"

"Physics!" Ben yells, and he launches his ball straight into the gutter.

"I know none of these people," Jaden says, and he passes his next turn.

I give speed bowling one try, and my ball ends up flopping backwards out of my hand and rolling behind me into Jonah's bowling bag. Oops.

Then Jonah decides to do speed bowling one better, by throwing *two* bowling balls down the lane at once. And then a manager comes over and asks us to leave.

"I should've known this was gonna happen," Jaden grumbles as we change back into our regular shoes. "Remember the winter carnival last year?"

"If they didn't want us throwing blocks of ice at each other, they should've made a sign," says Jonah.

"Or the Strawberry Festival in fifth grade?"

"Again. A sign. 'No whipped cream on the moonbounce.' It's not that difficult."

"I think there should be whipped cream on every moonbounce," Ben says, in what I think is supposed to be a sexy voice, but 1) there's nothing sexy about what he's saying and 2) he mostly sounds like he needs some Claritin. Jaden tries one more time.

"Summer before third grade. With the—"

"That was Rachel's idea!" Jonah interrupts. He turns to me. "Are you ready, Meghan? Let's get out of this place of deceit, and lies, and people who know too much."

The two of us walk out together, talking about movies and cartoons and swapping gym class horror stories.

"Thanks for letting me tag along," I say.

"My pleasure, milady," he says in a fake British accent. "So what happened the summer before third grade?"

"I'll never tell. Now let's kick some Carroll arse."

#

Carroll's team crushes ours on the field. I mean, duh. I barely even notice, though, because we're busy in the stands singing about ragtime gals, and yelling about speed football and moving the ball with your MIIIIIIND. Dani looks over at me a few times and wrinkles her nose like she can't believe she ever used to hang out with me, let alone consider me a best friend. But for once, I don't care. I'm having a blast.

The Carroll band plays first, since they're the visitors, and they're even better than they were at the last competition. But when it's our turn, we march onto the field anyway, and when Colleen yells, "BAND, ARE YOU READY, BAND?" we all say, "YES, SIR!" and give our dumb little Motown show our best shot. Everyone makes it through the tricky parts in "I Want You Back." Jonah gets the pyramid right, for the first time ever. And we finish with "Signed, Sealed, Delivered," which ends with the dance line girls doing some serious butt-shaking, and the

Patriots fans actually give us a standing ovation.

Well, either us or the dance line girls' butts.

Back in the band room after the game, though, none of us can stop talking about it. We got a *standing ovation*. Jonah *rocked the pyramid*. And *no one fell down*.

"Before tonight," Mr. Coffman booms as we pack up our things, "you guys were just a band. Now, you're a FORCE TO BE RECKONED WITH."

Everyone cheers, and I realize, he's right, maybe even more right than he knows. This was the first time I played the show without worrying about whether an ex-friend still liked me, or whether a bully with eternal PMS was going to yell at me. I marched onto that field knowing I belonged.

Finally.

CHAPTER THREE

A few days later, we're playing through "Reach Out I'll Be There" in class, and we're almost at the second verse, where the trombones actually get the melody for once, when Mr. Coffman cuts us off. Most of the band stops more or less on time. But Jonah's head is buried in the music, to the point where part of me starts wondering if maybe he needs a new prescription for his glasses, and he launches right into the trombone feature. He plays three whole measures all by himself—then he finally realizes nobody else in the whole room is making a sound except for him, and he stops, blushes, points to me, and says, "It was Meghan."

Mr. Coffman laughs and says, "Nice try, Reznik," and then starts in on the saxophones for lagging behind the beat. Meanwhile, I train my eyes on Jonah and his fake innocent smile, put down my trombone in as ladylike a fashion as I can manage, and then steal his music.

"Dude, give it back," he yelps.

"Not until you admit you're the one who screwed up," I say.

Jonah reaches for the paper, but I wave it out of his reach, like I'm teasing a kitten with a shoelace. "I told you, you have to say you were wrong first. And then you need to say you're sorry. And then you have to buy me a Coke after class. And then..." I lose steam and concentration, trying to think up something ridiculous for him to do, and he snatches the song back.

"Hey!"

Jonah tries that innocent smile on me again. But then he says, like a little kid reciting a poem or a prayer, "I screwed up. I was wrong. Meghan is a queen. No, wait, Meghan is a goddess. Meghan is the Goddess of All Things Trombone and we should all grovel at her feet. And if I make it out of class alive today, I will buy her a Coke."

"And one of those M&M brownies from the drama club bake sale."

"And two of those M&M brownies from the drama club bake sale."

"That's more like it," I say.

"I thought so," Jonah replies, smirking and placing the music back on his stand.

And then we just stare at each other, like we're in one of those staring contests everyone used to have in elementary school, where you're not allowed to laugh or smile or blink. Only this goes on way longer than a staring contest should, and no staring contest I was ever in before ever made my stomach do flips like this. Before I know what I'm doing, I find myself leaning forward a bit.

"Guys? Guys? Hello?" Brian waves his hand in front of our faces. Jonah and I blink and shake our heads in unison. We're both pink. It looks really good on him. Oh, my God.

"Welcome back, trombones!" Mr. Coffman says, opening his arms wide. "It's good to have you with us again. Now let's hear you from the pick-up to letter F."

And oh, yes. The whole band is looking at us. At me and Jonah, that is. Awesome.

By lunch time, there's a rumor going around that That Big Girl With The Frizzy Hair is hot for That Nerdy Kid Who Sits Next To Her In Band. By the end of lunch, the rumor is that Jonah and I were kissing in the middle of the band room, in the middle of class, and Brian had to break it up. By the time the fourth period bell rings, the rumor is that Jonah and I were having sex against the broken paper towel dispenser in the boys' bathroom by the D stairwell, and Mr. Coffman walked in and caught us. And by the time it gets back to me again at the end of the day, it's about two people I've never even heard of, so I figure I'm off the hook for now. Which is especially good, because in this version, Mr. Coffman doesn't so much *catch them* as *join in*. EW EW EW.

But then, after school, Rachel corners me on my way out the band room door and says, "Dude, do you have some kind of thing for my little brother?"

And honestly? I have no idea what to say. So I laugh and hope it sounds convincing. Wait—"hope it sounds convincing"? No, I laugh and it is convincing. Because it's true. It's totally laughable. Wait—what?

"Good," Rachel continues, rummaging in her bag and pulling out a flier on a bright orange piece of paper.

"Because we're having this family Halloween party next Saturday, and I want you to come. There's gonna be a campfire, and my mom's gonna bake too much stuff, and my dad's gonna play folk songs on his stupid guitar, and it's all gonna be so wholesome we'll be barfing up unicorns and rainbows for the rest of our lives."

"Okay, sure," I say, because to me, that kind of sounds like the best Saturday night ever, and I reach out my hand to take the invitation.

As soon as my fingers graze the paper, Rachel pulls it back with a flourish. "BUT," she says. "BUT, before I can give you this invitation, I need you to promise me that you're not gonna do anything weird."

"Weirder than barfing up unicorns?"

"Meghan, I'm serious. Tell me you're not gonna do anything weird, like having sex with my brother on the trampoline."

I blush, and my stomach starts flipping again, and it takes a few tries to get words out of my mouth. When I can talk again, I say, "Nah, the trampoline'll be too uncomfortable. I was thinking maybe one of the couches in the basement." And it must sound enough like a joke, because she finally hands me the invitation.

Well, of course it sounds like a joke.

Because it is a joke.

Right?

"Hey, Rach—Meghan! There you are!" Jonah appears out of nowhere, and oh, my God, please tell me he didn't hear anything Rachel and I said. He maneuvers around his sister and presents me with two M&M brownies. "Please accept these brownies as a token of my esteem," he says in his fake British accent, and where does he even get this stuff...and why is it making my heart all jumpy like this?

"What the hell is that about?" Rachel asks me.

Before I can explain, Jonah notices the invitation in my hand and scowls at his sister. "I told you, I was gonna invite her in band."

"Well, did you?"

"No," he admits. "I got...distracted."

I glance at him, he glances back at me, and then I remember 500 things I need to look for in my backpack, like, right now.

When I look back up, Rachel's giving me the squinchy Reznik face. "Whatever. We have to get to our bus." She turns and walks away. Jonah follows her. But he waves goodbye first.

#

The night before the Rezniks' party, Nina comes home to spend the weekend telling us why everything we do is wrong. And the weird thing is, Mom and Dad take it. When Nina won't eat the steak dinner Dad's fixed, because now she's a vegetarian all of a sudden, Dad apologizes and offers her a salad. When Nina leaves after dinner to meet up with some friends, and Mom says, "Be home by midnight," Nina says, "I don't have a curfew anymore," and Mom says, "You're right. See you when you get home." It's like she's a guest. No, not even a guest—a customer. Someone they can't be themselves in front of. And Mom and Dad don't yell at anyone else, either. Not me. Not Ellie. Not even each other.

But then, on Saturday afternoon, she announces that, before she goes back to school, she's going to drive out to Ocean City to visit Gram. And Mom and Dad explode.

I'm holed up in my bedroom when it happens, working on my first big English term paper and waiting for Rachel's friend Ilana to pick me up for the party, but even with my door closed and the Ultimate Trombone Playlist blaring in my earbuds, I can't avoid it.

"You're going to do no such thing," Dad says.

"I'm 18 years old. I can do what I want, and I want to see my grandmother."

"No, sweetheart, you don't," Mom says.

"No, Mom, *you* don't."

Whoa.

"Excuse me?"

"You're afraid of watching your mother die. That's why you're letting her stay out in Ocean City instead of getting her hospice care out here."

"What?" Dad yells. "Young lady, you will not talk to your mother that way."

"Yes, I will," Nina says. I can't see her, of course, but she sounds calm. Creepily calm.

"The hospice nurse is taking good care of her," Mom says. "She's stable, and she's comfortable, and it's good for her to be at her home, with all her things, and all her friends…"

"She should be with her family," says Nina, "and you know it."

The front door slams, and I watch from my window as Nina storms outside. Downstairs, Dad snaps something about introductory psychology class bullshit, and Mom says, "You know it's best for her to stay out there," but I don't know who she's trying to convince.

I put down my copy of A Raisin in the Sun and turn up the playlist, letting a whole brass section blast into my ears in stereo. Stupid Mom and Dad and their stupid argument about how her car is still in the shop, and whether his car can make it to Ocean City next week, and whether Dad gets to have the car because he has go into the office and it's his car in the first place, or whether Mom gets to have the car so she can see her DYING MOTHER, or whether Dad can't take a damn weekend off work every once in a while and help support his wife and help take care of his mother-in-law, and how can Mom expect Dad to take off work, even on a Saturday, when they've got three kids, and one's already in college—and not a cheap one, mind you, and what the hell was wrong with going to Salisbury anyway, it was good enough for Dad—and the other two are going to be in college before we know it, and God knows they're not gonna get scholarships like Nina did.

And maybe Nina was right, maybe there's something to that introductory psych bullshit after all, and if Mom really cared about her mother, then maybe her mother wouldn't be three hours away being taken care of by a total stranger.

A Trombone Shorty song comes on, and suddenly, I remember the Christmas in Ocean City a few years ago, when Gram handed me two packages and said, "These books weren't around when you needed them. The lady at the bookstore said they're both pretty new. But think of them as belated presents for Little Meghan." They were picture books: *Trombone Shorty*, and *Little Melba and Her Big Trombone*. They're still in my bookcase, under a bunch of other stuff, and I dig them out and page through them. Only Gram would have been able to get away with giving me those books, and only Gram would have known just how perfect they were.

Outside in the driveway, Ilana honks her car horn. Finally. "Bye, everybody," I call over my shoulder as I sprint out of the house. I don't know if they hear me. I don't care.

"Hey, Meghan," Ilana greets me when I open the car door. "You ready for some fall fun?"

"Anything to get me out of my house."

"And into Jonah's house," she says slyly.

"What?" I suddenly get very interested in pushing the preset stations on her car radio.

"I heard that rumor about you." She waits a beat. "You, Jonah, and Mr. Coffman."

"EW!" I squeal. "God, I thought that was over. Maybe we need to turn back, and I can hide under my bed until graduation."

"Seriously, don't worry about it. Nobody thinks you like Jonah."

"Really?" I'm not sure what to think about that, but the radio's playing a song I loved in first grade, so I turn it up loud, louder than my loudest thoughts, and we sing along until we make it to Jonah's house.

Jonah and Rachel's house.

The Rezniks' backyard is swarming with people—mostly adults I don't recognize. "Stick close to me," Ilana whispers. "Keep your head down, and avoid all eye contact. Otherwise, you'll have five hundred random moms wanting to know where you're planning on going to college."

I do what I'm told, and we arrive in the basement in one piece. All the kids are congregating there. Jonah, Ben, and Jaden have managed to take over the couches, the stereo, and the TV at the same time—stinky boy feet all over the furniture, nerd rock on the stereo, and an old *Simpsons* Halloween special on the TV. Bart and Lisa are in the library, trying to find a spell that will destroy zombies, and Bart's reading out what Nina once told me is actually a list of condom brands. I don't know how she knew that. I don't know why I'm standing here in my best friend's basement thinking about condoms, either.

Jonah jumps up and goes, "Meghan! You're here!" and then sits back down awkwardly as the other guys mumble hello through mouthfuls of Mrs. Reznik's homemade donuts. On the other side of the room, a bunch of little kids are playing their own version of Candy Land, while a boy who's a little bit older is whining, "NOOOOO! That's not how you DOOOO IIIIIIT! Rachel, make them play it right!"

Rachel appears, doing everything but turning her head backwards to avoid making eye contact with the annoying kids, and hugs both of us. "Estrogen!" she cries. "Adolescent estrogen! I'm so glad to see you both!"

Ilana and I exchange wary glances, which of course Rachel catches. "Sorry, you guys. Jaden and Ben have been here this afternoon, and my mom's friends all dumped their kids down here like two hours ago and said, 'Here, Rachel, why don't you find something fun for the little ones to do,' like it's my fault they're not old enough to entertain themselves." She looks back at the Candy Land game and shudders. "I didn't even know we *owned* Candy Land."

Rachel uses her older sister status to force the guys to make room for us on the couches, and unbelievably, it works. I end up squished between an armrest and Jonah. Ilana raises her eyebrows at me from across the coffee table. I stick my tongue out at her, and Jonah intercepts my face and makes an even worse one at me, but then I realize how close his hand is to my leg, and suddenly I can't move anymore.

The *Simpsons* episode ends, and Rachel swaps it out for an old DVD of this British show she and Jonah love, *Monty*

Python's Flying Circus. The Rezniks swear it's genius, but I can never understand what anyone's saying or what's going on. And whenever I do start getting into one of the skits, a guy in a suit of armor will come in and hit all the other actors on the head with a rubber chicken, or the whole show will switch into a weird cartoon.

Right now it's one of those cartoon bits, and there's an old statue with a fig leaf in front of its…you know…*parts*, and a cartoon hand keeps sliding in front of it and trying to take the fig leaf away. Everybody else is laughing. Usually, I'd be laughing, too. But I can't stop thinking about Jonah's hand. It's still right there, right next to my leg. So close it's almost touching me. So close it would be touching me if either of us shifted the tiniest bit…and then Mrs. Reznik comes downstairs. The cartoon hand yanks the fig leaf away, Jonah jerks his hand away from my leg like he's just realized it's attached to his body, and Mrs. Reznik orders all of us upstairs and outside for the campfire and s'mores.

Jonah and the other guys stampede upstairs (mentioning food is always a good way to get teenage guys to do anything you want them to do), the little kids pull Rachel along with them, and Ilana and I follow behind them. At the bottom of the stairs, Ilana pauses and says, "So how's the view from that tree up there?"

"What are you talking about?" If there's such a thing as a squinchy Riggins face, I'm giving it to her right now.

"The tree. Where you're sitting with Jonah. K-I-S-S-I-N-G," she sing-songs, and she turns around and heads upstairs before I can kill her.

Upstairs, it looks like my jacket's probably buried under a pile of other coats in the living room, and I'm searching through them for it when someone taps me on the shoulder. It's Jonah, and he's holding my jacket. I didn't even know he knew what my jacket looked like. For one insane second, I think he's about to help me put it on, or something, but instead he tosses it to me and says, "Come on, let's go outside."

Everyone's gathering around the campfire. Jonah heads instead for the trampoline, and I follow him. We sit down next to each other, stretching our legs out and pressing our hands against the trampoline to bounce up and down a little bit.

"I'm so glad you came," he says to me.

"Me, too," I say.

"Especially after that...stuff everybody was saying."

"About me and Mr. Coffman, right? Yeah, we were, um, hot and heavy for a while."

It's a stupid, stupid joke, but I need to make a joke, or something's going to happen, and I don't think I'm ready for something to happen. Am I?

"Ha," says Jonah—the actual word, "ha"—and for the first time I start wondering if he's as mixed up as I am.

We sit in silence for a minute or two, while the group near the campfire sings along with Mr. Reznik's guitar. It takes me that long to realize I'm staring at Jonah, and the cute little freckle at the corner of his smiling mouth, and as

I start shaking myself out of it, I realize I don't have any reason to get embarrassed. Because Jonah's staring back at me, just as goofily, with that giant smile on his face. I get that flip-flopping feeling in my stomach again, because it's just like that day in the band room. Except with one difference: this time, there's no Brian to break it up.

No Brian to break it up...

We both figure it out at the same time, and suddenly I'm in the middle of my third kiss. And for the record, it's way nicer than either of those kisses from Brian last fall. I take back everything I've ever said about all boys smelling bad —I'm sure plenty of them do, but right now, all I can smell is Jonah, and he smells like Irish Spring soap and the spices in his mom's apple cider, and even the boy smell hiding underneath those things isn't half bad after all. And maybe it's the Simpsons episode and my empty stomach talking, but I think I'm convinced now that the chewing gum and breath mint industry should give it up already, because you know what's really awesome? Kissing a boy who tastes like homemade cinnamon donuts.

We pull apart a bit, just to catch our breath. He pushes a curl behind my ear. "I'm glad we did that," he says, trying to sound calm. "Let's do it again."

I start giggling at his fake business-like voice, and how I can tell he's trying not to laugh, too, and then we're both laughing and kissing at the same time, and wow, forget all the dumb people spreading their dumb rumors at school, because this is kind of the best thing that's ever happened.

When we pull apart this time, Rachel is standing in front of the trampoline, staring at us with her arms folded. "Your kids are gonna look like hobbits," she says, and walks away.

"Cool," says Jonah. "You okay with that, Meghan?"

I find myself grinning. "You know, I think I am."

CHAPTER FOUR

Jonah calls me at home the next day, right around lunch time. My mom yells from downstairs, "Meghan, it's for you. It's some boy. Don't stay on too long, in case the hospital calls."

Of course, my first thought is, Jonah's calling to say he was possessed last night and I can't ever tell anyone he made the mistake of kissing me. Instead, he says, "Hey, Meghan. You left your phone here last night, and I think we should go out."

"What? Go out where?" I ask, and when I realize what he's talking about, I kick myself for being so stupid.

"Um." I can almost hear him making the squinchy face over the phone. "I meant, like, go out, go out."

"Oh. Um. Yeah." I'd say more, but my face is too busy seeing how big it can smile.

"I mean, we could go out somewhere, too. Like, today? I could bring your phone with me. Wanna go get lunch? Or dinner? Or an early breakfast so we can get a head start on tomorrow?"

"Are you allowed to go out on school nights?" Is that a stupid question?

He pauses. "Actually...I don't know. I guess I need to ask my parents. I guess I should probably tell my parents."

I can't picture telling my parents I'm going out with Jonah. These days, I don't tell my parents anything.

"I'll check, and I'll call you back, okay?"

"Okay," I agree, and hang up.

There's a knock at my bedroom door, and for a second I think maybe it's Mom, wanting to know who the boy was, and maybe I'll tell her about Jonah, and how maybe-just-maybe I all of a sudden have a boyfriend. Not that we've ever been that kind of family. But still.

From the other side of the door, Nina asks, "Can I come in?" and opens the door without waiting for an answer.

I haven't seen her since she left the house yesterday evening. Even by the time I got home last night, close to midnight, she wasn't back yet. I'd started to think maybe she'd left for good.

Nina moves a stray blanket over and sits down next to me on the bed. "I wanted to say goodbye before I go," she says. "I talked to Gram's nurse, and she said I could come out this afternoon. Gram's...mostly stable. For now." Her voice cracks a little as she says this.

"What does that mean?" I ask.

"I...don't really know," Nina admits, and hearing her say that is terrifying.

I think back to that last time we hugged, back at Gram's house over the summer, and I wish I were brave enough to hug her again. I'm not used to reassuring my big sister. I'm not used to doing anything with my big sister. "I wish I could come with you," I say. As scared as I am of seeing

Gram again, it feels like the right thing to say. It feels like the right thing to do.

"Me, too," Nina says.

"Tell her I love her," I say, trying not to choke on the words.

Nina gives me a tiny half-smile, and I can see that she's tearing up, too. "I will."

And then the phone rings again. And even though I'm sitting in my room now, with the phone on my lap, Mom still gets to the downstairs phone first. "Meghan! It's that boy again. Five minutes, tops."

I seriously need my phone back.

"Is everything okay?" Jonah asks when I answer.

I think about telling him what's going on. But he and I have only been officially going out for, like, twenty minutes, so it may be a little early to start sharing the dysfunctional family woes. Also, Nina's still sitting right there next to me on my bed, not even pretending she isn't listening. "Some things are better than others," I say.

"Would Chinese food at Jade Palace be a better thing or a worse thing?"

"Better," I answer immediately. "Definitely, definitely better. When?"

"As soon as humanly possible? I haven't had lunch yet, and there's nothing left in the house but graham crackers from the s'mores."

I've already had lunch, not that I had much of an appetite with Mom and Dad around. But I don't care. "I can bike there in like 15 minutes."

Nina's smiling at me when I hang up. "Who was that?" she sing-songs, like we weren't just talking about our sick Gram and our messed-up parents.

"No one."

"No one?"

"Someone."

"Someone?"

"Jonah," I say finally. Even saying his name makes my heart go loopy.

"Have fun," she says.

"Be safe," I say, and this time, I do hug her.

I grab my purse and my jacket, head outside, and get on my bike. I think I hear Mom yelling something at me as the door slams behind me, but I can't deal right now. And anyway, I've got a date.

Jonah's sitting on the curb outside Jade Palace by the time I pedal up on my bike. I wonder if I can kiss him hello —I would really, really like to kiss him hello, and then kiss him how are you, and nice to see you, and do you wanna split some egg rolls—but before I can decide, he jumps up, tosses me my phone, and says, "Whoo-hoo! Let's eat!" It's not a romantic sentiment, but it's one my stomach suddenly agrees with.

Jade Palace isn't much of a restaurant—it's mostly take-out, with a few little tables crammed into a corner—but it's near the playground Mom used to take us to when we were little, so Jonah and I walk over there and spread our lunch out on a picnic bench.

"Rach and I used to come here all the time," Jonah says, digging into his egg rolls.

"Us, too," I say. "We used to bring our lunch and have picnics." I don't remember that until the words are out of my mouth, but it's true. Before Ellie started preschool and Mom went back to work, we used to do that, like, every week.

"Remember when they had that little playhouse over there?" Jonah points to an empty corner of the playground. "That's where we used to play Cinderella Versus the Power Rangers."

I almost spit out a mouthful of orange chicken. "What?"

"Well, I always wanted to play Power Rangers. And Rachel always wanted to play Cinderella. So our parents made us figure out how to play it together."

Even when Nina, Ellie, and I were little, we didn't play together on the playground. Nina would swing on the swings, I'd build castles in the sandbox, and baby Ellie would try to eat bugs.

"Is Rachel okay?" I ask. I know "your new boyfriend's sister" is probably not on anyone's list of Romantic Things To Talk About On Your First Date, but then, the Power Rangers probably aren't, either. And Rachel's still my best friend. And after that hobbit comment, she didn't say another word to me all night. Not even goodbye.

Jonah considers this over a few bites of fried rice. "She will be. We just have to make sure she isn't around when we do this." He puts his chopsticks down and kisses me.

I look behind me, under the picnic bench, and inside the mostly empty take-out containers. And then I kiss him, too.

#

Nina texts me later that night: "Couldn't do it. Just drove back to school. I'm scared, too."

Jonah texts me, too: "XOXO. SWEET DREAMS."

#

There's a part of me—a dumb middle-schooler part of me—that thinks having a boyfriend will change everything. Like, I'll suddenly be popular, and school will get easier, and my family will get saner, and everything will be all hearts and flowers and crap.

So, yeah, that doesn't happen.

If anyone sends out a memo that says, "Meghan Riggins has a boyfriend now, so please treat her like she's a human being," I'm pretty sure nobody reads it. Most people, honestly, don't care. (And I guess I don't care about most of their love lives, either, so I shouldn't be upset.) Charlie and Colleen think it's the cutest thing they've ever seen, and that gets old kind of fast. Mom and Dad, when they're around and paying attention to me, call him That Boy. As in, "Stop slacking off and spending so much time with That Boy, or you'll never get into a good college." And seriously.

College. Is. Three. Years. AWAY.

Anyone else who cares wants to make some comment about what a loser I am for dating a newbie. And mostly, I can ignore it. But then, one Tuesday, when I'm a little late to after-school practice, Dani bumps into me in the locker room and says, all fake-sincere, "Oh, good, Meghan, I'm glad you're here. I thought you might be too busy baby-sitting." And she cracks up like it's the funniest thing she's ever said. Which it probably is.

I want to ignore her, too, the way I've been ignoring everybody else. But this is Dani, who used to be my best friend. Dani, who's breaking weeks of silent treatment so she can make fun of my sweet, funny, and completely adorable boyfriend. I slam down my trombone case, my nails dig into the palms of my hands, and in a voice I don't even recognize, I ask the question I should've asked a long time ago: "Dani, what the hell is wrong with you?"

She wrinkles her nose at me like I'm something disgusting she's stepped in. "I don't know what you're talking about."

I want to let that stop me, but I can't. Not now. "Is it 'cause Jonah crashed into you at the Carroll game? Or are you still mad at me 'cause Maya told you to be, back in September? Or—or are you a bitch? And it took me 'til now to figure it out?"

Dani's staring at me now, open-mouthed, like she can't believe what I said. That makes two of us.

I don't wait around for her to answer, because I know

she's not going to. Instead, I walk out of the band room, with as much dignity as you can have when you've just told off your ex-best friend, and the palms of your hands are probably bleeding, and also you're carrying a trombone case. I don't know what's happened here, but it feels good.

The thing that's hardest to deal with is Rachel. At lunch, or any time it's just us (which, okay, it usually isn't anymore), everything's fine. As long as I don't say anything about her brother. Which is really, really hard. But the rest of the time...Like, when she can tell Jonah and I are messaging each other, she'll start blowing up our phones with messages in our three-way thread, about some dumb thing that happened in ceramics class, or some movie we need to see, or pictures of cats who look like David Bowie. Or whenever I come over to their house, she'll open the door and block it with her body and say, "So are you here to see me, or are you here to hang out with *him*?"

So not everything gets automatically fabulous once Jonah and I start going out.

But a lot of things do.

It's awesome to have someone jump out of their seat when you get to class, because they're that excited to see you. Or to have someone's hand to hold on the way back from band practice. Or even to sit together on the bus, hanging out with our friends and pissing off everybody on the bus by singing cartoon songs, or dumb camp songs from when Jonah and Ben went to Jewish day camp together, or 101 variations on "My Darling Clementine."

(Brian even gives up in the middle of "Bohemian Rhapsody" one week because he can't hear himself over us.)

And the stuff that happens at his house after school, when his parents are working and Rachel's got art club, that stuff is kind of pretty great, too. Great...and confusing.

Like, the first time we have the house to ourselves, I'm pretty sure I'm not ready for anything but a little kissing. But then suddenly we're on the couch together, and our arms and legs are tangled up together, and my arms are pulling him down on top of me, and I don't know who's telling my arms to do that, and I'm wondering if it's the same person who figured out how to get Jonah to make that amazing sound he just made. Before anything else can happen, though, Jonah blurts out, "Meghan, I want to Wait." I know what he's talking about. I can even hear the capital letter in his voice. But I still say, "Wait for what?" and he says, "You know. Wait. I mean, I'm pretty sure. I think." While he's biting his nails over it, I turn purple and make a weird guffawing kind of noise as if it's the furthest thing from my mind. Which, fine, is a total lie, because it's RIGHT IN THE MIDDLE OF MY BRAIN, in flashing neon lights, but now that he's brought it up, I'm remembering that I'm supposed to Wait, too. I mean, I *want* to Wait. I mean...

It's kind of impossible to think rationally in our current position. I straighten back up. "Okay," I say. "I get that. I mean, I do, too. I want to wait. I think. So, what do we do?"

"What do we do?" Now he's confused.

"I mean…should we should stop…kissing?"

He looks shocked. "No! No! I think we should keep kissing. I think we should kiss, like, all the time. But…"

"But?"

"But we should be careful, is all."

"Careful," I repeat. "Careful is good." And I pull his hand away from his mouth and kiss all of his fingers. Carefully.

But the next time we're alone together, we ditch the basement for his bedroom.

And the time after that, both of our shirts end up on the floor.

Maybe we're not so good at careful. But maybe careful is overrated.

#

Ilana and Claire are the last ones to get to the Rezniks', and the only ones to arrive in costume. Ilana's Sally from *The Nightmare Before Christmas*, and Claire is some kind of Goth Alice in Wonderland. "None of you dressed up?" they say, wrinkling their noses at us and our normal-people clothes.

"Dressing up is for babies," Jonah says.

"Bullshit," says Rachel. "Last year you went trick-or-treating as Commander Riker from the old *Star Trek*."

"I did not," he says, but I can tell from his eyes that he totally did.

"And he took his trombone with him. And instead of saying 'trick or treat,' he'd get it out and play the *Star Trek* theme."

"I did not!"

"You totally did."

He sighs. "I totally did," he admits.

"Loser," Ben laughs at him.

"You're one to talk," says Jonah. "You were dressed as Wesley Crusher."

"It was ironic!" Ben lunges for Jonah, Jaden intercepts them, and Rachel says, "Hey, idiots, we better get going."

"So you see now," she says to me as we walk up the stairs, "how sexy that boyfriend of yours is."

"Yes," I say. "Yes, I do."

At the haunted house, we join a huge line of DHS and Barbara Fritchie kids. I notice Dani and Maya ahead of us, standing with a bunch of other clarinets and drummers. The girls are all dressed as babies, complete with pigtails and pajamas and stuffed animals and painted-on freckles. The guys are all dressed as "bums"—flannel shirts and old jeans, aka what they usually wear, but on Halloween, they get candy for it. Dani catches sight of me and whispers something to Maya, and they look back at me and cackle. A month or two ago, that would have crushed me. Even after I told her off in the locker room, it still hurts a little. Like, wasn't she listening to anything I said? Didn't it matter to her at all?

Maybe it only mattered to me.

And maybe *that's* all that matters.

So instead of crying, or hiding, or losing myself in dumb memories of middle school, I turn to Jonah and ask, trying to sound casual, "You ever look back at your life and wonder why you used to be friends with people?"

"I've been friends with Ben since I was three," Jonah replies. "I do that every day." He takes my cheek in his hand, and turns my face away from Dani, until my nose is touching his and all we can see is each other. "Just ignore her," he says. "Just look at me. Look into my eyes. Look into my nose hairs. Check me for boogers."

"Ew," I giggle. "God, what are you, eight?"

"Just the right age for a babysitter."

And we kiss until we make it to the front of the line.

Inside, the haunted house is divided into four rooms, and none of them have anything to do with the Civil War after all. One has some people in vampire costumes going, "I vant to suck your bloooooood," while strobe lights flicker on and off and some rubber bats drop down from the ceiling. The next has a mannequin in a Frankenstein suit lying on what looks like an old dentist's office chair, while a dude in a lab coat yells, "IT'S ALIVE! IT'S ALIVE!" and more strobe lights go on and off.

In the third room, they've turned off the lights, taken a bunch of old shelving units from one of the stores, covered them with sheets, and arranged them like a maze. It's so dark, we think the room is empty, until hands start reaching out from holes in the sheets and poking us. In front of me and Jonah, one hand grabs Rachel's ankle. She kicks it away with a loud thwack, and then there's an even louder "OW!" from behind the sheet because Rachel's wearing her Doc Martens today. And when I'm readying myself for a sneak foot attack, a hand comes out around the level of my chest. Before I even know what I'm doing, I whack the hand away with my purse. The shelving unit under the sheet starts wobbling, and Jonah tries to steady it with one arm while putting his other arm around me. "Are you all right?" he asks. Before I can answer, the shelving unit lands on the floor with a loud crash, taking out the hundred-year-old boom box that's been blasting the "spooky" sound effects.

"That's it, you're outta here," says a guy in a werewolf mask, emerging from behind one of the sheets. We stare at him.

"All of you!" he yells. "Get out now!"

We take off and run straight to the exit through the last room, which appears to have nothing in it but a glass case full of teddy bears with glowing eyes.

"You know," I say to Jonah once we're back outside, "that makes two places I've been kicked out of since I started hanging out with you. I don't know what to think about that."

He grins. "Only two so far?"

I nod.

He squeezes my hand and says, "Then we've got some work to do. How do you think Putt-Putt feels about speed mini golf?"

CHAPTER FIVE

Homecoming is kind of a big deal.

Maybe it's not like that in normal towns, where actual *stuff* happens, but in Dulaney, it's like Christmas and the county fair in one, if part of both Christmas and the county fair was hating on Fritchie, our Homecoming rivals. The whole week before Homecoming is Spirit Week, and we're all supposed to come to school looking even dumber than we normally do (Pajama Day! Twin Day! Wacky Hair Day! '80s Day! Blue and Gold Day!), and whichever class looks the dumbest all week wins the prize of having the most embarrassing yearbook pictures to show their future kids, or something. And Monday through Thursday we've got marathon band practices, trying to get the full show on the field and make it look good enough that no one will throw food at us from the stands. Then, Saturday, it's the parade, the game, and the dance. And the end of my first marching band season.

So here's the thing about parades. In case you haven't noticed before, they're long. And when you're marching in them? They're really long.

Take the Macy's Thanksgiving Day Parade. Gram loves it, because it reminds her of when she was growing up, and her whole family would bundle up and go see the parade together. So every Thanksgiving morning, when we're visiting her in Ocean City, she wakes us up early so we can watch it with her. When I was little, I didn't mind so much —I always liked the balloons, and I loved the Rockettes— but once you get to fifth grade or so, you don't know who any of the balloon characters are anymore, and you realize all the Rockettes are like 80 years old.

So think about how long it takes to get through a parade when you're just watching it and can leave whenever you want to pee or hide out in the bathroom, and multiply it by, like, 20, and that's how long it takes to get through a parade when you're marching in it with a trombone.

We march the whole way across town to Fritchie, and during the whole parade we only play four songs: "I Want You Back," "My Girl," "Don't Stop Believing," and the fight song. Over and over again. By the time we get to the Fritchie stadium, I feel like I'm about to pass out. I can't believe we've got a whole football game to get through.

What's worse, all I can think of, besides my stupid achy body, is how much I wish Gram was here. I'm wearing her claddagh necklace, for the first time since Columbus Day weekend. Until today, every time I've taken it out of my jewelry box, I've ended up putting it right back in. Having it around my neck would be like a reminder of everything that's going wrong, when I'm desperately trying to pretend that everything's all right. But today, all I know is, I want her here with me. I want her cheering me on in the stands, I want her helping me get ready for the dance, I want her to know I'm with the cute freshman now.

Jonah notices the necklace when we're in the stands, taking off our hats and loosening our jackets until halftime. He brushes my hair away from my neck and then carefully touches the claddagh charm. "Shiny," he whispers, and I know it's a high compliment.

"My gram gave it to me. Before...before she got sick."

He takes my hand. "How's she doing?"

"No change. That's what they say, anyway."

"Okay." He knows that I don't like talking about it. So he slips his arm around my shoulders, and we sit quietly together while everyone around us screams at the football field. And then it's halftime.

We march onto our field and play our hearts out, and while a few people (fine, including me) slip a little in the mud, we all stay upright. We march through all four songs, we nail our trombone feature in "Reach Out I'll Be There," and Jonah even does all right with the pyramid. It's really a nice way to end our season—even though I notice, as I'm scanning the stands at the end, that my family is nowhere in sight.

Mr. and Mrs. Reznik pick Jonah, me, Jaden, and Ben up, and we pile into their minivan and head over to the Reznik house, where we meet up with Rachel, Ilana, and Claire from the art club. We're gonna hang out for a while, then head to dinner at Red Robin (Classy? Maybe not. Delicious? Absolutely.), and then hit the Homecoming dance. I think for the hundredth time about how cool it is, even though it made things weird when Jonah and I started going out, that Jonah and Rachel are *friends* besides being brother and sister, and their friends all get along with each other, and their parents are always willing to have some or all of us over at their house. Especially since we're always eating all of their food and taking over their TV. This afternoon we decide on *Monty Python and the Holy Grail*, and I guess I finally drank the British comedy Kool-Aid, because today, it's the funniest thing I've ever seen.

After the movie, we split up. The guys stay downstairs, take all of five minutes to get ready, and then spend the next hour or so arguing over the rules of some confusing board game. We girls head upstairs to Rachel's room, and even though none of us are the girliest of girls, it still takes until the guys have vanquished the evil wizard, or collected all the sheep, or vanquished the evil wizard sheep, for us to be ready.

Claire and Ilana, who are going to Homecoming together, went out last weekend and bought these weird old dresses at one of the vintage stores downtown. Claire found a '60s minidress and white go-go boots, and Ilana's wearing what she tells us is a flapper dress from the '20s. Rachel's also going retro, in a red velvet dress with bell sleeves, paired with a huge cameo choker.

"There's no such thing as the '90s revival," Claire says. "Everyone in the '90s just dressed like it was the '60s."

"You're just mad that my dress only cost ten bucks," Rachel says.

"You're right."

I'm the only one who isn't treating the night like a time-travel costume party, but I still look decent. My dress is black and knee-length, with spaghetti straps and a swirly skirt that'll hopefully distract people from my giant boobs (or at least that's what one of Ellie's magazines said). And I'm wearing the earrings Gram gave me for my birthday last April, before everything went wrong, as if that'll make everything better again.

Back in the basement, we find, the guys are wearing...black suits. But Jaden's tie has music notes on it, Ben's has astronauts floating in space, and Jonah's has zombie pirate robot ninjas. While everyone's standing around chatting, Jonah and I sit down together on the basement steps, apart from the rest of the group.

"Nice tie," I say, taking it between my right thumb and index finger and pulling him closer.

Jonah grins. "I spent two days trying to figure out whether I was a zombie guy, a pirate guy, a robot guy, or a ninja guy, and it turns out I never had to choose in the first place. What a world we live in." Then his face turns serious, and he moves even closer to me on the steps. "You look..."

"Weird?" I supply, not missing a beat.

He flushes my favorite shade of pink, and then says low in my ear: "Amazing."

Jonah has warned me about a hundred times that he doesn't dance, which is mostly fine with me—I just want one or two slow dances to prove to the world that I really do have a boyfriend, and in the meantime, we can hang out. As soon as we get inside the gym, Jonah and I run into Charlie and Colleen, who are hanging out with Kenzie, Dean, and A.J. It feels like the beginning of band camp all over again, except for one thing.

"Where's Brian?" I ask Charlie, while Jonah's talking to Dean about some nerd-rock band I guarantee Dean's never heard of, even if they do have a "kickass trumpet player."

Charlie shrugs. "He said he wanted to start practicing for All-State auditions."

"They're not for, like, two months."

"You know Brian," Charlie says. But maybe I don't, not anymore.

That song about people's butts comes on, and Dean starts dancing, and Kenzie and Colleen team up to make fun of him for "dancing like a dad." If their plan is to get him to stop dancing, it fails spectacularly, because the stupider their dance gets, the stupider his gets, and pretty soon we're all trying to out-stupid each other. Which of course is something Jonah can totally get behind, so he starts dancing, too.

And when the next slow song comes on, and I say, "Please, Jonah? Let's dance to this one," he's too wiped out to argue. I settle my arms around his neck, and he places his on my waist. I think about last month, fumbling around on the dance floor with Brian, and I think about how right it feels tonight with Jonah.

Gram told me once that back when she was in school, the nuns who'd chaperone the dances would carry rulers around with them to make sure all the couples were standing at least a foot apart. But judging from all the bumping and grinding going on around us, there aren't any nuns in our gym tonight. So as the song goes on, I press a little closer to Jonah. And then a little more. And, okay, a little bumping happens, too. And here's about where a sitcom character in my place would make a stupid joke about Jonah being happy to see them.

Even in the dark, I can tell Jonah's turning pink again. I think just about every part of me is flushing, too. He pulls away just a bit and asks, "Uh, do you wanna go take a walk?" His voice goes up about two octaves on the last syllable. Which, weirdly enough, makes me want to get closer to him again.

So we walk hand in hand out of the gym, through the crowded cafeteria where all the cliques are getting their pictures taken, through the dark, empty hallways, and finally to the closed door of the band room. We can still hear the bass line booming from the gym speakers.

"Hey, wanna see if the door's open?" I say, mostly kidding. "We could go in and put up fake names on the Sousa Award plaque. Or something."

"Or...something," Jonah says, grinning wickedly. My heart does a pretty fantastic freefall into my stomach.

He tries the door. It's open. We head inside.

At first, we just stand in front of the band locker room

door. Then we find out it's still open, too. "I can't believe Mr. Coffman forgot to lock up," Jonah says.

"Well, it's Homecoming," I say. "He probably had a lot on his mind." And then I can't wait any longer, so I put my arms around his neck and pull him close, and we kiss our way inside. Jonah presses me up against the wall of lockers. He's still very, very happy to see me.

Before I can think myself out of it, I pull off his jacket, brush aside his tie, and start unbuttoning his shirt. I kiss his first freckle, the one by his mouth, and then his second, which hides below his left shoulder blade. He eases the straps of my dress down my shoulders, wrestles with my bra clasp, and leans down to kiss the skin he's just uncovered.

I find myself thinking back to that first conversation in his basement, about being careful. But like I said, being careful is kind of starting to feel overrated. So when I cup the front of his pants with my hands, to see what will happen, Jonah sucks in his breath so hard I see that old agreement of ours fly right out the window. He pulls away slightly, fixes me with a look, and slowly slides his hands under my dress. I shiver a little bit, and not just because I've been losing my clothes.

Maybe I should be freaking out about what we're doing. But I don't think I can stop myself, and I wouldn't want to if I could.

"So," Jonah says, a little out of breath. "Maybe...forget everything I said about...you know...waiting."

The voice in my head—the one I've gotten so good at ignoring—says something I don't feel like listening to at the moment. And I can't really hear it over my heartbeat, anyway.

"Fine by me," I say, also out of breath, and I unzip his zipper and start to pull down his pants, just as the door opens.

"Oh. Oops."

I pull my dress up, Jonah yanks his pants up, and we look up to see Charlie and Colleen standing in the locker room doorway, looking almost as mortified as we are.

"Sorry, guys," Charlie says.

I've never been more pissed off to see Charlie in my life. But then, maybe I've never been happier to see Charlie in my life, either.

The four of us stare at each other, and then at the floor, and then Jonah and Charlie get really interested in the Funky Winkerbean posters on the opposite wall, and Colleen says, "Bathroom. Meghan? Come with me?" So I do.

"Sorry about that," she says while we check our hair and re-apply lip gloss. "Did we totally fuck up your night?"

Yes, I think.

"No," I say. "I mean…it wasn't a good idea. I mean, we'd never—and we didn't even—oh, God."

"You're probably right," she says. "Your first time should be somewhere nice. And the band locker room smells like drummers."

"So what about you and Charlie—"

"Oh, it's okay for us. We're gonna break up after tonight. We just wanted to do it one more time before we dump each other."

"You're...breaking up?" There are a lot of things I want to ask Colleen about what she's said, but this one seems the safest.

"Sure," she says, shrugging. "I mean, we're graduating in like seven months. I've gotta start concentrating on college stuff. And it wasn't supposed to be a long-term thing, anyway. It was just supposed to be for the marching season."

"Oh." I'm not sure what to say to this, either. "And that's...all right with you?"

She shrugs again. "Why not? He's cute, and I knew he liked me. And the sex..."

Oh, God.

"The sex is, like, AMAZING."

Oh, my God. I do not want to hear this...do I?

"Seriously, Meghan, I don't know if it's a trombone thing or what, but that boy's got *skills*." She hugs herself, and then twirls around. Her dress has a swirly skirt just like mine.

We meet the guys back in the hallway, which is beginning to fill with other couples, other groups. The dance is over.

Mrs. Reznik drops me off at my house, after what will probably go down as the longest and most awkward car ride in history. We're barely out of the parking lot when Rachel goes, "Where *were* you guys?" I go through a long list of possible answers, each of them worse than the next, and finally say, "We ran into Charlie and Colleen," as Jonah says, "Band stuff." Whatever that means. Then Rachel goes, "Where?" and Ben goes, "Band stuff? What band stuff? Why wasn't I invited?" Jonah and I can't say anything. We can't even look at each other. But he squeezes my hand as I get out of the car, and he says, "Talk to you tomorrow?" and I let myself in the house with my key.

Mom, Dad, and Ellie are sitting in the living room. All of their eyes are red.

"Meghan," Mom begins, but tears keep her from getting any more words out.

"Gram died today," Dad says. "While you were at Homecoming."

CHAPTER SIX

We get up the next morning before the sun even rises, and drive all the way to Ocean City. Nina is already there. We stay in the house—Gram's house—with Uncle Eddie, Aunt Liz, and their little kids, Henry and Nora. The adults make plans for the funeral, arguing about the readings and the hymns, who should be the Eucharistic ministers, who's going to be the pallbearers, what's the best way to get to the funeral home, where are we having dinner after the wake, who's staying with the little kids during the funeral.

Nina slumps in Gram's favorite chair with her psychology textbook open on her lap. Ellie watches a marathon of one of those teen soaps where all the girls end up pregnant. Not exactly what I want to be seeing right now, but the noise on the TV is better than the noise inside my head, so I sit on the couch next to her. Henry and Nora, who are six and four, wander in and out of the living room, looking for someone to pay attention to them. They don't know what's going on—they only know Gram from Christmas, and Nora kind of seems to think Gram is married to Santa Claus.

I keep my phone in my hand, like at any second I'll know exactly what to say to Jonah, but every time I go to turn it on, I freeze, and the reception's crap out here, anyway. I spend most of my time flipping through Gram's photo albums. I think back to the last time I saw Gram, and how I ran out of the hospital room like a coward and never got to say goodbye. Or I catch myself thinking about Homecoming, thinking about Jonah pressing me up against the lockers, thinking about his mouth on my neck and his hands inching up my thighs. I replay Homecoming night over and over again in my head, only in this version, Charlie and Colleen are nowhere in sight. But then Mom will sniffle, or Uncle Eddie will cough, or one of the little kids will start screaming, "That's miiiiiiiine! Give it baaaaaack!" and I'm jolted back to reality with an extra shock of guilt.

The morning of the funeral I wake up at 2:00 a.m., from dreams of Gram at the wake, lying there with her rosary beads in her hands, surrounded by flowers and wreaths from family and friends and half the Queen of Angels parish. One thought is pounding over and over again in my head: me wanting to have sex with Jonah made Gram die. This goes on for about half an hour until I force myself back to sleep.

Then I wake at 3:00 a.m. convinced Gram died because I spent most of fall semester avoiding my family.

And then I wake up at 5:00 a.m. convinced I killed Gram because I was too scared to spend time with her in the hospital.

I wonder if this is what people mean when they talk about Catholic guilt. I wonder if you can still have Catholic guilt if you only go to Mass on Christmas and Easter. I wonder if Gram's dead because we didn't go to church enough. I'm having trouble breathing now.

I try to talk myself down. None of these things killed Gram. Cancer killed Gram.

Cancer killed Gram.

Gram is dead.

#

In the morning—the real morning—it looks like nobody else got much sleep, either. Mom and Dad, Uncle Eddie, and Nina are drinking black coffee out of chipped "World's Best Grandma" mugs at the kitchen table. Aunt Liz, with her hair still wet from the shower, is trying to coax Henry and Nora out of their sleeping bags. Ellie is snoring on the couch next to a half-eaten bowl of Raisin Bran.

The adults have decided the little kids should stay home today, with Ellie to "take care of them." The rest of us get dressed. I'm wearing my Homecoming dress, with a black cardigan of Nina's over it—it's the only black dress I own right now, and I haven't even washed it since the dance, and I hate myself for wearing it. I put on the claddagh necklace, and then remember that I was wearing it at Homecoming, too—and then I hate myself even more.

Queen of Angels is dark, and with all the rain outside, the stained glass windows aren't letting any light in, either. I can't remember if I'm supposed to bless myself with the holy water on the way in or on the way out, or if I'm supposed to make the sign of the cross with it or make the crosses on my forehead, lips, and chest like Gram does at the Gospel. Like Gram did at the Gospel. So I bury my head in my purse until we pass them, and then we all file into the first pew together.

It's weird to be in the front at church. Gram's favorite pew was closer to the back, where she could see everything that was happening, so I'm used to having a whole congregation to rely on when I forget what happens next. I try to fumble my way through all the standing and sitting and kneeling, and through all the prayers I only say once or twice a year: "God from God, Light from Light"; "Heaven and earth are full of Your glory; hosanna in the highest"; "only say the word, and my soul shall be healed." We sing Gram's favorite hymns: "On Eagle's Wings," "I Am the Bread of Life," and "Amazing Grace."

Mom reads the Prayer of the Faithful, and when she gets to the line about Gram, and says, "For Your servant Elizabeth," she chokes up too hard to keep going. She stands there for a few seconds just breathing, wiping at her nose and eyes, and then Dad comes up to the lectern, puts his arm around her, and picks up where she left off: "For Your servant Elizabeth, who in baptism was given the pledge of eternal life that she may now be admitted to the company of the saints, we pray to the Lord." And we say in unison, "Lord, hear our prayer."

Afterwards there are hugs from relatives I don't

recognize and old ladies I've never met before, and then there's a lunch at a seafood restaurant near the boardwalk, but I can't get myself to do much more than mush up some crab cake pieces and push them around on my plate, so eventually I excuse myself, bundle up in the too-small winter coat Gram gave me for Christmas last year, and take a walk.

I've never seen the boardwalk so empty before—even at Christmas time, there are people wandering around, trying to escape their families for a little while. I walk past souvenir shops with tacky t-shirts still hanging in the windows. Past the Ripley's Believe It Or Not! museum with the giant shark crashing into the wall; past Playland, all but the Ferris wheel hidden and shuttered; past Gram's favorite saltwater taffy stand, the one she always visited before coming to see us.

I think about all the summers I've spent here. Every Thanksgiving. Every Christmas. I think about Gram driving in for our birthdays every year, for Nina's graduation, Ellie's soccer championship, the All-County competition. I think about leaning over the pit with her at *The Nutcracker.* "This is my granddaughter. She just picked up the trombone herself. She's going to be a star."

Nothing's ever going to be the same again. Nothing's ever going to be good again.

I watch the waves and a few dumb seagulls who haven't figured out it's November yet, and then I walk back to the restaurant, where my family is waiting.

PARADE REST

CHAPTER ONE

Jonah and I break up on Monday. And it's all my fault. And it sucks.

When we get back from Ocean City, there's three voicemails from Jonah on our home phone.

"Hey, Meghan, it's me—"

Delete.

"Hey, Meghan, did you lose your phone again?"

Delete.

"Hey, Meghan, call me back when you can?"

Delete.

I know I should call him back. I want to call him back. But I'm not sure what to say, so I cross my fingers that I'll figure something out before band on Monday morning.

But I don't. I meet with Ms. Ramos first thing to talk about about making up the English test I missed the day of the funeral, and by the time I get to the band room and take my seat, Mr. Coffman's already warming the band up, and Jonah's too busy with scales for me to have to talk to him. For me to talk to him.

With Homecoming over, marching band season is over, too, and we switch to concert band mode to prepare for the Winter Holiday Concert with the freshman band and the school chorus in December. A Winter Holiday Concert, as I learned back in middle school, is basically a Christmas concert, except that every group also includes one Hanukkah song, and the chorus usually sings a song about world peace. We sight-read something called "Joy to the World," and we get more than halfway through before Mr. Coffman finally realizes that it's not the Christmas carol, it's the old rock song about the bullfrog. Then Colleen passes out a medley called "A Hanukkah Celebration," and all I want to do is joke with Jonah about why "My Darling Clementine" wasn't included. Instead, I turn to my left and ask Brian about All-State auditions.

When class is over, and we're packing up, Jonah catches up with me on my way to the band locker room, takes my free hand, and says, like he did the day after his family's party, "Is everything okay?"

I want to lie to him, so, so badly. I want to tell him everything's fine, and go sing stupid songs and quote Monty Python sketches and make fun of trumpet players. I want to go over to his house and make a stop-motion Hanukkah movie with the trombone part to "I Had A Little Dreidel" as the soundtrack, and then sneak up to his bedroom with him and lock the door. I want a hundred things, and all of them are Jonah, in a world where nobody's dead, where nobody's ever died before. But I can't have those things anymore. And I can't tell him what's happened, either, because if I tell him, I'll have to relive it all. I'll have to watch his face fill with concern, and hear his voice go all sympathetic, and I don't think I can do that and stay in one piece for the rest of the day.

So instead I tell him the two true things I can tell him without completely falling apart. I say, "I love you," and I say, "I'm sorry," and then I run out of the classroom. I spend lunch in the girls' bathroom, writing Jonah a breakup note. Thesis statement: I'm really sorry, but I think we have to break up. Supporting paragraph one: I think we have to break up, because I really suck. Supporting paragraphs two and three: I think we have to break up, because I really, really suck. Conclusion: I'm sorry, I'm sorry, I'm sorry. Ms. Ramos would be proud. I feel sick.

But breaking up with Jonah via five-paragraph essay isn't the worst part. The worst part is, I don't even give Jonah the note myself. I make Rachel do it for me.

It's a shitty, shitty thing to do—and I know it as I'm doing it. Rachel lets me know it, too. When I meet her at her locker after school, before she can say anything to me, I hand it to her and say, "Listen, can you give this to Jonah? And, like, not read it?" But of course she opens it anyway. And she only needs to skim it for like a second to figure out what's going on. She balls it up and spits out, "You used me to get to my brother, and now you're using me to get rid of my brother? Fuck you." Those are the last words she says to me, and every single one is a punch in the gut.

I don't see Jonah again until band the next day. He's late this time—and I'd know even if he didn't sit next to me, because my whole body's turned into a Jonah detector, and I can't concentrate on anything until I know he's here, until I know what's going to happen.

Jonah sits down next to me, starts greasing his slide, and strikes up a conversation with Nicky Zukosky on his right. Mr. Coffman calls us to attention.

If this is what I wanted, then how come it hurts so much?

And it doesn't stop hurting. And it hurts for a hundred different reasons. Every time I see him out of the corner of my eye (I can't look him in the eye anymore), I think about all the time I wasted hanging out with him, watching bad movies and arguing about cartoons, when I should have been living in the real world. And even worse, I think about Homecoming, and I think about Gram, and I hate myself for being so stupid, for being such a dumb hormonal teenager. And worst of all, I still like him, so, so much, and if I'm not careful, the memories of Homecoming night still flip my stomach and turn my heart upside down.

I guess Ben and Jaden are in charge of cheering Jonah up, because they're not talking to me anymore than Jonah is. Or Rachel. Or even Ilana and Claire.

That's fine with me. I don't want to be around most people anymore. I want to stay home, and do my homework, and set the table every night, and hope nobody else dies. I practice trombone a lot, more than ever, and Chip must notice, because he makes me send in an audition recording for All-State band. And the chance of getting to skip town for a weekend in Baltimore, away from my family and my ex-friends, is too good to pass up. Brian and I show up early to school on the day Mr. Coffman gets the results, and when we find out we've both gotten in, Brian actually hugs me. Since I've broken up with Jonah, whatever weirdness there was between me and Brian has vanished. And thank God, because as long as I'm chatting with him, I don't have to look on my other side and see Jonah there.

After the winter concert, which is maybe only two steps above being a total embarrassment, we're supposed to turn in all our music to Colleen, who's holding court in the music library. What I don't know until I walk into the room is that Kat is helping her.

Kat hasn't bothered me since the Potomac competition, but I'm still not looking forward to spending any one-on-one time with her. So I try to toss my folder on the folding table and get the hell out of there as fast as I can, but then, as I'm walking out the door, she says, and I quote, "Hey, I'm sorry I yelled at you that one time, now leave us alone so we can file this shit."

Wait, what?

Back in the band room, Charlie's still sitting in his seat in the back row. I figure he's waiting for Colleen, but when he sees me, he pounces. "So, Kat talked to you, right?"

"Huh?"

"Kat apologized. Right?"

Then me and my brilliant brain figure it out. Of course

Kat didn't apologize out of, like, the goodness of her heart. Kat probably doesn't even have a heart. Where Kat's heart is supposed to be, there's probably a sign that says, "CONDEMNED." "Oh, God. What did you tell her?"

"Nothing," he protests, but I haven't seen Charlie this uncomfortable since Colleen made him section leader, so of course I know "nothing" means something, and I'm about to press him, when he admits it. "Fine. We had a meeting yesterday—the section leaders and the drum majors—to talk about the season and stuff.

And, like, some of us might've talked about upperclassmen bullying the newbies and how they should apologize. The upperclassmen. To the newbies."

"You mean Kat. To me."

He shrugs. "You weren't the only one, you know. But, yeah, you're the one I was talking about. So Colleen and I did tell Kat she should talk to you. And she did. Right?"

"As much as she's ever going to," I say. "You guys really didn't have to do that."

"Yeah, we did," Danny says.

"Thanks," I say.

And that's how the semester ends.

#

School finally lets out for winter break, and if I think the last month and a half sucked, it's nothing compared to Christmas at home, without Gram. Dad works all

Christmas Eve and the day after Christmas, and I'm betting he'd work all of Christmas Day, too, if he didn't think Mom would kill him for it. Mom takes us to Christmas Eve Mass at Holy Family, a church we haven't set foot in since Ellie was baptized, and the priest gives an anti-abortion homily that sends Nina storming out to the car, where she waits for us until the service is over.

Ellie wakes us all up early Christmas morning, like nothing's wrong, but she's the only one who cares about what's underneath the tree. I get some clothes that are too small, a pair of earrings I would never wear, and Selected Studies for Trombone. Nina drives back to Pennsylvania right after breakfast, Dad disappears into the den, Ellie hides in a corner playing games on her new phone, and I sit in the living room with Mom and watch *White Christmas*, just like we used to do with Gram, and I cry.

#

The day after Christmas, I brave Boscov's to exchange some of the things that don't fit. I'm not especially interested in going home, and it's one of those weirdly spring-like winter days we get every once in a while in Maryland, so I get a hot chocolate from Baltimore Coffee & Tea and walk around the shopping center. And that's where I run into Jonah and his new girlfriend.

When I catch sight of them, standing in front of the movie theater with their backs toward me, I can almost convince myself it isn't what it looks like. But then he puts his arms around her waist, and he smiles at her the way he used to smile at me, and then he's kissing her the way he used to kiss me, and she's standing on her tiptoes to reach his lips because even in her heels—her three-inch heels—she barely comes up to his shoulders. I think I'm ready to go home now.

CHAPTER TWO

All-State is the week after winter break. I try to put all thoughts of Jonah and his new girlfriend out of my head, but I do find out (by accident, not because I'm actively looking for info like a detective or a weird stalker girl or anything) that her name is Lizzi Cohen, and she's a freshman who goes to temple with him, and she's not in marching band, she's in student government. And that's how they got together, because they're both on freshman exec committee, and they planned some stupid holiday food drive together.

It's all so wholesome it makes me sick. Or it would make me sick if I cared, which I totally don't, so there. It's a brand-new semester, and Jonah's back in freshman concert band while I'm still in the upperclassmen concert band, and anyway, I'm wrapped up in practicing, and packing, and texting back and forth with Brian, who's taking jazz band instead of concert band this semester, to "broaden his horizons," and trying to convince me to do the same.

Since I made All-State and broke up with Jonah, my parents have eased up on the getting-into-a-good-college lectures. (Yeah, they've replaced them with new lectures, about how I should try to get a music scholarship. But somehow I don't mind those as much.) The Friday that

All-State starts, Dad actually volunteers to take a few hours off work so he can give me a ride into Baltimore. I set my alarm for 5:30 a.m., which I'm pretty sure should be illegal, but before my alarm goes off, something much better wakes me up. The scent of Dad's pancakes.

When my sisters and I were little, Dad made pancakes for us every single Saturday morning. Sometimes he'd make them into shapes, or he'd add some sausage or bacon, or maybe he'd break out the juicer and do homemade orange juice. And we'd all crowd into our tiny kitchen and eat together. That stopped around the time I hit middle school, when he started working most Saturdays, and I hadn't realized until now how much I'd missed it. And it gives me about enough energy to shower, get dressed, and throw my suitcase and trombone into the car. Then Dad starts driving, and the traffic and the public radio DJs lull me right back to sleep, until we finally pull into the hotel parking lot.

It's chaos inside—carloads and busloads of kids are swarming into the lobby, lugging instruments and choir folders and squealing at each other from across the room. By the time I finally find the band check-in table, get my room assignment and a huge folder full of all the rules and regulations we're supposed to follow this weekend (and seriously, if any of us actually sit down to read them, we won't have time to do anything else), and make it all the way up to the fourteenth floor to drop my stuff off in my room, it's time for our first rehearsal.

The first thing I notice about All-State Band?

I'm way out of my league.

I can tell from the minute I walk into the hotel ballroom. Even warming up, everybody sounds like pros. And then I start hearing bits of conversation between the scales and lip slurs. "Yeah, I just got in early decision to Oberlin." "I'm waitlisted at Ithaca." "Peabody." "Eastman."

Brian's second chair, and I'm sixth (out of six; go figure), so we have about enough time to wave across three other kids at each other before practice gets underway.

Our conductor is Dr. Taylor, who directs the band at Seton College. Chip knows her, of course, through what Brian calls "the Music Teacher Mafia," and ever since we found out I made it, Chip's been telling me stories about her at our lessons. The time she told a timpanist who'd been slacking off that she could replace him with the first guy who sat down in the audience...and then she did. The time she got so into conducting An American in Paris that she whacked herself in the face with her baton and broke her nose—and kept conducting. Everyone else must have heard the same stories, because all she has to do is step up on the podium, and the entire room falls silent. She reminds us that we should all be warmed up already, because we don't have any time to waste (oops), and she starts yelling at us from the first measure of the first piece, and she doesn't stop until we break for lunch. And the funny thing is, the more she yells at us, the better we sound.

Lunch is in the hotel dining room, and even the fancy tablecloths and chandeliers can't hide the fact that the food's no better than the crap at the school cafeteria. I sit down next to Marin, the girl playing fifth chair trombone, and a few other girls, Varsha and Heidi, from the chorus. It turns out they all go to Guilford Hall Prep, one of those fancy Baltimore private schools where everybody makes All-State and everyone gets into Harvard. When I tell them I go to Dulaney, Marin asks me if everybody there is in a gang and I have to carry a gun, and Varsha says, "Dulaney? I thought there was nothing out there but cows." I say, "No, the cows all died out in the last gang war," and everybody looks at me like I've got two heads and maybe a third arm, too. I'm pretty sure none of these girls are gonna be my new best friends.

But they're nice, anyway. Marin, especially. It's cool to meet another trombone girl—or, you know, one who isn't Kat. She talks a lot, and by the end of lunch, I know she's a total classical music nerd, her family has season tickets to the Baltimore Symphony, she crushes on the guy who used to conduct the Concert Artists of Baltimore, and she and her brothers have a brass quartet that plays at weddings and church services. I'd feel like a total fake if she weren't so sweet. And if she didn't tell me about fifty times over the course of lunch that she was feeling like a total fake herself, compared to everybody else.

"I mean, the first chair guy, Miles? I've known him since we were like five? He's going to Oberlin next year. Like, it's already been decided."

"Wow."

"And that guy playing second chair?"

"Brian?"

"You know him?"

"Yeah, he's a friend of mine," I say, because it's less complicated than saying, "We're in band together, and I talk to him to avoid my ex-boyfriend, and also he kissed me twice."

"WOW. I mean, have you listened to his tone? Did he always sound that good? Who does he take from? Where's he going next year? Wait, how is he only a junior?" And on and on until I'm almost expecting her to ask me to get her an autograph. From Brian.

Brian sounds amazing. I've gotta admit that. I've never really heard him play anything but our easy band music before, so maybe that's why I didn't know how good he's gotten. When we get back to the ballroom, he and Miles are playing at each other. Brian's improvising a jazz solo, and Miles is scoffing, "Oh, jazz. I was into that for a while, but now my private instructor wants me concentrating on classical repertoire." He pronounces "repertoire" with a ridiculous French accent, and then he starts playing orchestral excerpts from Bolero on his mouthpiece, so Brian starts improvising on his mouthpiece, and even though they both sound like sick mosquitoes, Brian's mosquito may sound the healthiest. Or something.

But no matter how good he sounds, Brian's still Brian.

We're working on this piece *Second Suite in F*, by Gustav Holst—the third movement, "Song of the Blacksmith"—and Dr. Taylor's chewing out the poor drummer who's playing the anvil. Yes, the anvil.

"So, Meghan, I never told you, congrats on dumping Jonah's ass," he calls over the clanging.

Awesome. "Um, can we not talk about that right now? Or, like, ever?"

"Okay, what do you wanna talk about?"

"I know," says the guy playing fourth chair. "You can talk about how not to get the whole trombone section in trouble with Dr. Taylor."

The third chair girl says, "Yeah, you know what happened to that guy who played first trombone at Seton two years ago, right? He was talking in the middle of rehearsal, and she threw a pencil in his eye, and now he's blind."

"That didn't happen," Brian says, and goes right on talking to me. "Hey, guess what? I'm buying a new trombone. Well, an old trombone. An antique Conn. And it's in great shape."

I'm also pretty sure that story's made up, but I still kind of shield my eyes with my hand when I answer. "Dude, you're such a brand snob. You made it in here playing a Bundy. The Conn's not gonna make any difference."

"You're playing a Bundy?" Miles says. "Are you ten?"

"See?" says Brian. "The Conn's gonna make all the difference. I'm a serious musician now, man. I need serious equipment."

"Serious equipment, huh?" I ask, and once it's out of my mouth it sounds like the dirtiest thing I've ever said. But it's just Brian. And he's just a friend.

"Oh, I've got your serious equipment right here, baby," he says, and of course it's loud enough that Dr. Taylor finally hears us.

She bangs her baton on her music stand for order. "Trombones. Enough."

Everyone turns around and looks at us.

"See?" says the third chair girl, all pissy.

Brian and I stare at our music, because if we look at each other, we'll lose it.

"Anvil, let's try it again."

Clang, clang, clang, clangy-clang.

"So how's that 'serious musician' thing going?" I ask Brian, still staring at my music stand.

Clang clang, clangy-clang-clang.

"Go to hell, Meghan."

"No thanks," I say, "I hear it's full of anvil players."

Clang, clang, clang.

#

We're not allowed to leave the hotel under any circumstances—not that I could get anywhere without a car, anyway—so they've come up with mandatory fun for us to have each night we're here. Friday night, we're all herded back into the ballroom after dinner for an ice cream social. I guess the point is we're supposed to meet the kids from all the other schools, but mostly everyone sticks to their school cliques. For a little while, I hang out with Brian, and we talk about music and stuff. Then Miles comes over, and the two of them start fighting over whose trombone has the biggest mouthpiece or whatever, so I go hang around on the edges of Marin and her friends for a while, but they're all talking about what someone said to someone else at some Guilford party, and there's nothing I can add to that, either. So I finish up the last of my soupy ice cream, toss my Styrofoam bowl in the garbage, and take the elevator back to my room.

Supposedly I have a roommate for the weekend—her name's Gabi, she's from Randallstown, and she's singing in the chorus—but all I've seen of her so far is the suitcase on her bed. They assigned our rooms alphabetically, and I'm betting she's crashing in a friend's room instead of taking her chances with a stranger. If the point of All-State is that we're supposed to make friends and meet new people, it's not exactly succeeding. For me, anyway. I stretch out on my bed, turn on the TV, and flip through the channels, trying not to feel homesick. Or Rachel-sick. Or Jonah-sick.

Around 10:30, there's a knock on my door, and I'm pretty sure murderers and rapists don't usually knock, so I answer it. It's Brian.

"Meghan, where did you goooo?" he asks, pushing past me and flopping onto the bed—my bed—without even asking if he can come in. I should be annoyed, and I should also be reminding him that guys aren't allowed in the girls' rooms, but mostly I'm glad I'm not alone anymore.

"Where did I go?" I repeat. There's not much room for me on the bed, so I perch on the free corner Brian's left me.

"Downstairs, at the ice cream thing. Why'd you leave?"

I shrug. "I was full."

"We should talk some more," Brian says. "We haven't talked, like, all day." But instead of talking, he finds the remote and starts clicking through the channels, finally settling on one of last summer's superhero movies.

"Can't you go bother Miles or someone?"

He looks genuinely surprised. "Am I bothering you?"

I have to think about that one. Is it worse to be depressed by myself, or annoyed with Brian? "No," I finally answer. "Not so much, anyway."

"God, I love this movie," Brian says, satisfied. "Remember that part with the lasers, when they're all like p-CHOO! p-CHOO! p-CHOO! And then the guy's like 'AAAAUUUUUGGGHHH!' And then—"

And then?

And then, I turn off the TV and kiss him.

Maybe I want him to shut up. Maybe I want my brain to shut up. Maybe his tone really is that good, and I really am enough of a band nerd that that, like, does something for me. It doesn't matter, though, because he's kissing me back, and man, is he better at this than he used to be. I wonder if Brian's kissing me because he likes me, or because I kissed him first, or because anything's better than being downstairs at that dumb ice cream social. And I wonder if, if I kiss him hard enough, I'll finally be able to stop thinking about the last person I kissed like this.

I keep wondering, we keep kissing, and then there's hands, and they're in places, oh, my God— and it isn't until I roll over onto the TV remote, and accidentally turn on the TV as the lasers start p-CHOO-ing, that I finally come to my senses. "We'd better stop," I say. "I'm sorry. This is a really, really bad idea, and you better go back to your room before we get in trouble. In like, 100 different ways."

Brian looks hurt, but then, once he's readjusted all the clothes that need adjusting, he says, "I've got a girlfriend, anyway. Which you'd know if you hadn't stopped talking to me for two months." And he walks out the door.

What the hell is wrong with me?

#

"What's up with you and the second-chair cutie?" Marin asks during a break in our Saturday morning rehearsal. "You guys are, like, totally ignoring each other today. Did he finally get scared of Dr. Taylor, or what?"

I know I probably shouldn't say anything, but I feel like if I tell somebody, maybe it won't feel so bad. "We kind of…hooked up last night," I whisper, hoping nobody else will overhear.

"How up?"

"Huh?"

"How *up* did you *hook*?" Marin asks, raising her eyebrows with every word.

"Um. Kind of up," I admit. Not quite as up as I had with Jonah, but way upper than I ever should've with Brian, that's for sure. I think I was wrong about this making me feel better. Actually hearing myself say it out loud, and having to relive it in my mind, and seeing the look on Marin's face, makes me feel like crawling into a hole for the rest of my life.

"Oh, my God. That's…Wait, is that a good thing? Or what?"

"It's a very, very bad thing. I'm an idiot."

"You are not an idiot. If he even looked at me, I'd probably drop my pants."

I burst out laughing. "You. Are. Insane."

"No more than you are," she reminds me. As if I needed to be reminded. "Hey, listen. Did you see what the evening program is tonight?"

I didn't. "It's gotta be better than the ice cream social… right?"

"Wrong," Marin says. "It's a sing-along."

"You've gotta be fucking kidding me."

"I so wish I was. Listen, Varsha and Heidi and I are gonna skip it, and we're gonna hang out in my room instead. You should come by. We'll keep you out of trouble. And if your friend over there comes by looking for you, I think I can figure out a way to distract him."

"Ew. Ew ew ew ew ew." And I've still got at least fifty more "ew"'s to go when Dr. Taylor calls us back to our seats.

#

After last night, I'm probably the last person who should be talking about logic. But it still seems a little weird to me that, in our quest to avoid the sing-along (or, as it's called in our info packets, a "POWER SING!"), Marin, Varsha, Heidi, and I spend the evening in Marin's room…singing.

The thing about choir kids—and I'm learning it this weekend, being cooped up in a hotel with like a hundred of them—is that, since they can't put their instruments away in cases, they never, ever stop singing. So even while we're watching TV and trying to figure out some complicated card game Marin wants to teach us, what starts as Varsha humming one of the chorus pieces under her breath quickly becomes her and Heidi playing some kind of dueling divas game and seeing who can sing "Defying Gravity" the highest and the loudest. Then someone in the next room bangs on the wall and yells, "If you kids don't shut up, I'm gonna have you kicked out of this hotel." Which would probably be inconvenient, since we have a concert tomorrow and everything. But Varsha's pouting. "Stupid old guy," she says. "I wanna keep singing."

"So sing quietly," Marin suggests.

"Sing a lullaby," I say.

And that's exactly what they do. Varsha says, "We did 'All The Pretty Little Horses' in chamber choir last year," and she and Heidi begin to sing, harmonizing together in their best quiet choirgirl voices. When they're finished, Marin says, "My mom used to sing that to me, too, but she did it a little different," and she sings the version she knows. And then I find myself saying, "My mom's not a singer, but my Gram used to sing me this one." And then I'm singing, "Hush, little baby, don't say a word, Mama's gonna buy you a mockingbird," and the other girls join in.

"That's so sweet," Marin says.

"Yeah. She was…pretty amazing," I say. Dammit, now I'm going to cry. And while I try not to, the other girls all watch me, in that sympathetic and awkward way you do when someone starts tearing up in front of you.

And then Varsha says, "Hey, I know. I started working on this one in my church choir last week," and without waiting for a response, she quietly starts to sing the perfect song. It's called "Wanting Memories," she says, by Ysaye Barnwell, but all I know is, it sounds like everything I've wanted to say to Gram since she died: how much she gave me while she was here, how much I miss her now that she's gone. Varsha sings the chorus through a few times, and soon we've all picked it up. Heidi begins to improvise a lower part, and once Varsha slides up to a higher part. Marin and I stick to the melody, giggling a little whenever one of us gets swayed by the other parts. The more we sing, though, the easier it is to listen to Heidi and Varsha without straying from the melody, to hold down our part, to blend our voices together. And the four of us sing together until the song is wrapped around us like a quilt, drawing us together and keeping us safe.

#

Sunday morning, we're loaded onto school buses to take us to the convention center downtown, where we're giving the concert. Amid all the other kids and parents crowding the hallways, I manage to find Mom, Dad, and Ellie. They hug me like it's been two years instead of two days, and wish me luck, and then it's time for the performance.

The high school band is the last group to perform, after the middle school band and both choruses. I kind of wish we could see the other groups, but Dr. Taylor's got us stuffed into a conference room while we wait. Marin and I try to play that card game of hers again, but somehow, it's even harder with two people than it was with four. Brian's still ignoring me, and I don't blame him. I'm ignoring him right back, and if I were him, I'd be ignoring me, too.

But then it's time for the performance. Which we rock. To the point that I can barely believe I'm one of the people making it happen. I forget about Brian, I forget about Jonah and Rachel, I even forget about how much I still miss Gram, and for half an hour, I'm nothing but my trombone and the music on the page and all around me.

And when the whole band plays those last few notes together in *Symphonic Metamorphosis*, I have one of those epiphanies Ms. Ramos is always talking about in English class: I never want to go back to the DHS band again.

After this concert, after this whole weekend, I can't go back to honking my way through whole notes in bad pop song medleys every day. I know what it's like to be a serious musician now, and I'm not going to settle for anything less. Not anymore. And since the phrase "serious musician" makes me think of Brian, before I screwed that up, I should admit that after what happened with him this weekend, I know more than ever that I have to avoid both him and Jonah. No. Matter. What.

It only takes a few days to figure out a plan and put it in motion. Instead of doing third-period concert band, I'm going to do an independent study. Chip assigns me all kinds of stuff to work on: technical exercises, lyrical studies, and most importantly, the audition repertoire for the regional music camp Dr. Taylor's running in the summer. Once my parents, Mr. Coffman, and the principal sign off, I'm all set. Independent trombone study every day, lessons with Chip every week, and maybe even summer camp to look forward to. It's gonna be awesome.

CHAPTER THREE

Independent study is rocking my world, and I don't care how nerdy that sounds. Third period is the best part of my day, and if I could skip out on all my other classes and spend the whole day practicing in the choir room, I would. Some days, I do skip going to the cafeteria for lunch, and eat in the classroom instead. It's not like I have anyone to eat with, anyway. Once or twice Charlie comes by on his way to the cafeteria, but I don't have much to say to him. I don't have much to say to anybody, these days. But hey, I'm getting great at reading tenor clef.

In March, the week before the camp auditions, Chip and I go over the audition piece one more time, measure by measure. By the time the hour's up, I'm exhausted.

"You're gonna do great, Meghan," he says while I'm packing up my things. "Let me know how it goes."

"I will," I promise.

I pick up my trombone and backpack, and as I'm about to leave, Chip says, "By the way, I'm starting with a new student right after you today. You probably know him, actually. He's got a lot of potential, too. I hope those teachers at Dulaney know how lucky are to have all three of you."

"All…three of us?" I say, my stomach sinking.

"Sure. You, Brian, and—"

The studio door opens.

"Jonah."

Because it's not hard enough to avoid him at school; now I'm going to see him every Saturday in Hagerstown, too.

"So you guys do know each other," Chip says happily, like he's honestly surprised that two trombone players at DHS might be aware of each other's existence.

"Yeah," Jonah mumbles, looking everywhere but me. "So anyway, Mr. Martin, I got that Arban book. I'll go ahead and get it out."

And he turns away without saying a single word to me. And I know I'm the one who started this whole freeze-out thing, but watching him give it right back to me hurts. A lot.

#

A week later, I borrow Mom's car and drive out to Seton College for the camp audition. I circle around the campus until I finally find the music building, and once I'm inside, I sign in with a Seton music major who wishes me "Lots of luck!" and follow the noise to the auditorium, where everyone's warming up.

It's funny how, a month ago at All-State, being in a room filled with musicians this good freaked me out. Today, it almost feels like coming home. I spot Marin warming up with some other girls near the back row, and walk right over to join them.

"Meghan!" Marin calls, waving. "Oh, my God, I am so nervous."

It's weird to say I'm not, so I don't. Instead, I compliment her dress, which is ankle-length and black and makes her look like a member of the Baltimore Symphony instead of a high school kid with crushes on inappropriate people. Meanwhile, I'm wearing a navy blue sweater and a flowered skirt, and I look like I'm on my way to my Confirmation.

Marin introduces me to the other girls, who all go to Guilford with her, but I forget their names as soon as she's said them. I'm busy scouting out the competition.

"Is what's-his-name here? Miles?" I ask.

"Oh, he's not trying out," Marin says, rolling her eyes. "He said no way he was gonna try out for a fake Interlochen when he could spend his summer at the real Interlochen."

"Oh, good Lord."

"No, tell her the best part," says one of Marin's friends.

"The best part is," Marin says, "he tried out for Interlochen. And he didn't get in."

Okay, that's kind of hilarious.

There's someone else I want to ask about, too, but I'm kind of afraid of the answer.

"Brian's over there," Marin says, giving me my answer anyway. "I went over and said hi to him when he came in, and he called me *Marie*. He's still a cutie, though."

"No, he's not," I say. But I can only think of one thing worse than spending the summer with Brian, and that's spending the summer with Jonah. So I say goodbye to Marin and head for a less crowded corner to warm up. And then it's time.

The trombones are auditioning in the science library—Guilford Hall is so rich that every single department has its own library. The walls are lined with shelves of textbooks and posters of plants and planets. Three people—two men, and one woman—are sitting at a long table, frowning. I remember hearing that the judges would be music teachers from different mid-Atlantic colleges, but I don't know who any of them are, and they don't look like they're going to tell me.

"Meghan Riggins?" asks the balding man.

"Yes," I say. Then I wonder if that doesn't sound professional enough, so I say, "Yes, sir." But the only time I've ever said "Yes, sir" in my life has been in marching band last semester, so it comes out way louder and more enthusiastic than it should. Go me.

His expression doesn't change. He continues, "Begin with a G major concert scale."

Phew. G major is one of the easier ones—only one sharp to worry about. I've practiced this one to death, and I can almost always do two octaves. I splatter a little on the high F sharp, but I don't think it's too bad. The judges scribble some notes down, and then the woman, without looking up, says, "B-flat concert scale."

Oh, crap. That high B-flat always kills me. And with that miserable performance on the high F-sharp, I'm not about to try hitting something even higher. So I remember Chip's advice, about it always being better to play a decent one-octave scale than a bad two-octave scale, so I play my pathetic one-octave, as quickly as I can, and then—shit—was that Chip's advice about scales, or was it "Better to play a slow two-octave scale than a fast one-octave scale?"

The judges aren't any help. They're not even looking up.

"Audition piece, please," says the white-haired guy, still scribbling down notes.

This I can do. And I do it pretty well. I remember all the dynamic stuff Chip and I have worked on, I nail the weird accidentals and the sixteenth-note runs in the variation, and I bring it home with the big dramatic ending. Whew.

And then there's the sight reading. The sheet music is already on the stand in front of me, turned backwards. "You have two minutes to study the piece, starting now," the bald guy says, so I flip it over and get to work.

And when my time is up, I fake my way through the piece as best as I can. They look up for a second and say, "Thank you," in unison, like robots. I wonder if maybe they are robots.

"When will we...um...know?" I ask awkwardly, and the woman says, "Two weeks," and then they go back to their notes. I guess I'm done.

#

The morning we're supposed to hear our results, I'm up refreshing my email at midnight—because midnight is technically morning, right?—and when I haven't heard anything by third period independent study, I email Chip. "Do you know if the results delayed or something? I've been checking my phone all day."

Chip writes back, "I got an email from Brian, and he heard he made it this morning. But you know, sometimes glitches happen. I'll check with Dr. Taylor and get back to you. I know you worked really hard on this one."

But later, after school's out, Chip sends me a new email. And maybe he's never heard of letting people down easy, because the subject is "Bad News." The email starts, "Well, there's a lot of competition out there," and ends, "There's always another audition! Don't give up!"

I have to read it a few times before it finally sinks in, but when it does, it sinks in good: I didn't make it.

FALL IN

CHAPTER ONE

It's all I can do to get through the rest of the week.

Chip tries to cheer me up with new goals for my independent study, like incorporating theory studies and music history, and, for the love of God, *writing assignments*— and I make it through about five pages of a Leonard Bernstein biography before I get so sick of reading about brilliant teenage Lenny hanging out with all his brilliant musician friends that I chuck the book across the choir room and knock over a trophy.

Marin texts to let me know she didn't make it, either, and invites me to Baltimore over the weekend so we can cheer each other up and maybe catch a brass ensemble performance at Peabody, where her ancient secret pretend boyfriend teaches. I still don't 100% get her taste in guys, but at least her taste in music is good.

Mom and Dad try to be sympathetic, but of course they don't really understand—and when they ask me to explain it to them, why it's such a big deal, why it matters so much, I can't come up with anything that satisfies them. Then they remind me that Nina's coming home next week, for mid-term break, and while she's here, I need to at least try and be pleasant.

I hate being pleasant.

#

On Friday morning, when I'm dropping off my trombone before the first bell, Mr. Coffman stops me and says, "So, Meghan, I heard from Chip about the camp audition. Any chance we can get you back in concert band for the rest of the semester? We could use a third trombone."

Oh. Great. Because the only thing better than going back to band, and Jonah, would be going back to band and being *beneath* Jonah.

I mean, *below* Jonah.

Good Lord.

"Um, no thanks," I tell Mr. Coffman. "I mean, I'm still really busy with independent study, and I've got these etudes to learn, and this book to read, and…"

He raises his eyebrows, unconvinced. But he doesn't challenge me. He says, "Well, the offer stands if you want it. The concert's not until May. And while we're on the subject, if you don't want to join us for concert band, maybe you'd be able to help us out with graduation band."

"Graduation band?" I repeat. "What the he—I mean, what?"

Mr. Coffman explains. "You know, this year's graduating

class is one of the largest we've ever had at DHS. So they're moving the ceremony from the gym out to the football stadium. And they've asked me and Ms. Lozaro to put together a little performance for the band. We'll have some newbies joining us, and we'll be practicing after school starting next month. Charlie won't be able to march, of course, so right now it's Jonah and two other freshmen, and I bet Jonah would love to have your help."

And I bet Jonah would take anyone's help before mine.

"Think about it, all right, Meghan?"

I do. For a second. And there's one thing I need to know. "Which one of us would be the section leader?"

Mr. Coffman blinks a few times, and then does that big, boomy, smiley thing he always does when he wants to avoid confrontation. "Let's not worry about that now," he says. "We'll all be working together! It's all about teamwork!"

"I'll think about it," I say.

But it's mostly to shut him up.

Mostly.

#

Up until now, whenever Nina's come back to visit, she's been pretty much the same Nina she'd always been. And when she gets out of her car, she still looks like Nina. But there's something different about her. It takes me until she gets into the house to realize what it is. She's smiling.

Nina starts talking as soon as she gets inside the house and doesn't shut up until she falls asleep. At least that part hasn't changed. By the time dinner's over, we all know all about how she signed up for a gender studies class this semester, as a requirement for her psych major, and how it's the best class she's ever taken, and how the professor's changing her life, and she's making so many amazing friends.

Then later that night, just as I've changed into pajamas, she knocks on my bedroom door, lets herself in and settles into my beanbag chair. "Let's talk, Meghan."

"Um," I say. "Okay."

Obviously, we've never been the kind of sisters who hang out with each other and have late-night soul-baring sessions. So I'm surprised enough that she wants to spend time with me—and talk with me—voluntarily. And I'm shocked when the first thing she says is, "Meghan, seriously, I have to thank you."

"For…what?" I have no idea what's coming next, but I'm definitely curious.

Nina takes what I guess is called a cleansing breath, and it strikes me that she's looking more relaxed than I've seen her…ever. Even when we were little kids. "Okay, listen. All I've ever done is work. That's all I've ever been good at. I study, I get good grades. And you know what? It hasn't done a damn thing for me. I'm always stressed. I'm always scared. I have anxiety disorders—did you know that? I tried to get Mom to take me to a therapist when I was in high school, but she said I just had to stop worrying so much. Which is exactly what my therapist is helping me do now."

"Wow," I say, because there's really nothing else I can say.

"But you...Ellie, too, but especially you. You guys have *lives*. You have things you love to do, and not just because they're gonna look good on a college application. I mean, I never, ever understood why you decided to play the trombone. But you had so much fun with it. And it got you into marching band. And you made all those new friends... you went to parties, you were in Baltimore...you had a *boyfriend*," she says, like I've somehow finally succeeded in forgetting. "You have no idea how lucky you are. You're the smart one, Meghan. Not me."

Add this to my new and quickly growing list of "Things I Never Thought I'd Hear My Big Sister Say."

"If I'm so smart, why didn't I get into camp?"

"If I'm so smart, why didn't I get into Brown?" Nina counters. "But I got into other schools, and I love the one I picked. So maybe it's not all bad."

"Maybe," I repeat.

Nina stands up and stretches. "Listen, I'm going out with some friends tonight, but I had an idea about something we could do tomorrow, if you and Ellie are interested."

"Yeah?"

"How about a road trip to Ocean City?"

#

We don't tell Mom and Dad what we're doing. It seems like too much, like it'll set them off, so we tell them we're driving into Baltimore to spend the day at the Inner Harbor. Instead, Nina navigates along the highways and across the Bay Bridge to Ocean City. The traffic's light, even along the bridge—of course, it's March, and even though it's spring break, it's not warm enough yet for the tourists to make the pilgrimage—but it still takes us almost four hours to make it to the cemetery.

None of us has been here since the funeral in November, but Nina remembers the way, so we follow her as she weaves through the gravestones to William and Elizabeth Murphy. Pop-Pop and Gram.

"What do we do now?" Ellie asks.

I roll my eyes at her out of habit, but honestly, I don't know what to do either. When Gram would take us to Pop-Pop's grave on Easter, we'd bring flowers along. Other graves are covered in grocery store flowers, American flags, stuffed animals. We didn't bring anything.

Nina unfastens one of the enamel pins from her bag—the one that says, "This Is What A Feminist Looks Like"—and places it carefully next to Gram's gravestone. She sits there quietly for a moment, like she's praying, or maybe listening. Then she turns to me and Ellie. "What do you want to tell Gram?"

Ellie runs her hand along the carvings in the gravestone,

and then sits down cross-legged in front of it. "I miss you," she says to the gravestone, like Gram's right there. "I've got my first softball game next week, and I wish you could come to it."

She stands up, and it's my turn. My sisters look at me expectantly. Maybe if I were a better person, I could do this in front of them, but instead I say, "Can I...I mean, can you guys...?" I wave toward the parking lot.

"No problem," Nina says, getting it immediately. "We'll meet you back at the car."

And when they're out of earshot, I sit down in front of Gram's grave and tell her everything. About Jonah, and Rachel. About Homecoming. About All-State, and Brian, and not getting into Dr. Taylor's stupid camp. About how much I miss her. I have nothing to leave her, like Nina did, so when I'm finished, I trace her name on her gravestone one more time. I'm too exhausted to do much else.

On the way back home, we stop at a diner off the beltway. Nina orders a plate of fries, and Ellie and I each get the turkey dinner platter, and try not to be disappointed when it turns out to be deli meat, lumpy instant potatoes, and cranberry sauce from a can. Dad's is so much better.

We don't talk for a while—we just poke at our food while some crappy country song whines in the background.

Ellie, of course, is the one who breaks the silence. "How come Mom and Dad never took us out here?" she wants to know. And once she's said it, I want to know, too.

Nina pushes the fries around her plate while she thinks,

and then she says, "Well, I don't know if you guys have noticed this, but…Mom and Dad aren't exactly good at… dealing with *life*."

"What does that mean?" Ellie asks, and all of a sudden, I'm so grateful for my little sister, who asks all the questions I'm too old to ask, that I could hug her. But I don't.

"Well, think about what happened when Gram got sick. Did they tell us about it? Not until they had to. And even once we knew, did we ever talk about it?"

"They yelled a lot," Ellie says.

"Mom and Dad are really good at avoiding things. Mom pretends nothing bad ever happens, and Dad hides at work, and they think that's gonna make the bad things go away. And then that doesn't work, so they yell until they think the bad things have run away," Nina says. "And it's completely unhealthy, because things *don't* really go away."

"What things?" asks Ellie.

"Any things," Nina says. "Gram being sick. Us having to worry about money. Me having—well, any things. You can't run away. You have to *deal*."

You can't just run away. You have to deal. Suddenly, I can't stop squirming in my seat.

"And I know Dad would say this is Intro to Psych bullshit," Nina continues, "because that's what he always says when I call them on it. But it's true." She pops a fry in her mouth and settles back into her chair.

I squish the mashed potatoes under my fork, watching

them ooze up between the tines. Ellie jiggles the straw in her soda back and forth through the ice cubes, splashing water everywhere. Then she asks another question. "Do you guys believe in heaven?"

Nina and I look at each other. I don't think either of us was expecting that one.

We're not a religious family. I mean, obviously. We've always done Christmas and Easter, because we always spent them with Gram. But we don't go to regular Sunday Mass, or Sunday school, or anything like that. We were probably all only baptized because Gram wanted us to be.

"Like, storybook heaven?" Nina asks. "With harps and wings and everything? I don't think I ever believed in that."

Ellie looks kind of wistful. "I know it's made up," she admits. "I still like thinking she's still out there, and watching us. You know?"

"Me, too," Nina says.

I think about that song Varsha taught us back at All-State, how the singer knows that the person she lost is still with her, saying the things she needs to hear. And I say, "I think she still is."

CHAPTER TWO

I don't sleep at all that night. There's too many conversations happening in my head. Everything Nina told me the night before, everything I said to Gram, everything my sisters and I said over dinner.

I put on Gram's claddagh necklace for the first time since the funeral, and then I dig up a pile of stuff that's been collecting dust in the dark under my bed for just as long. Some pictures Rachel took during her vintage camera phase: the two of us doing our best David Bowie impressions after we watched *Labyrinth*, me and Jonah practicing "My Darling Clementine" together, a group photo on Homecoming night. There's a few notes Jonah had stuffed into my locker—not even really notes, but little doodles and things he'd drawn in class for me. And then there's a list I made about a hundred years ago: "Reasons I Like Marching Band." I read it over, for maybe the first time since I wrote it, and then finally I know what to do.

\#

The first time I message Rachel, she ignores it.

The second time I message Rachel, I watch an ellipsis dance in the chat window for what feels like an hour, but then...nothing. Whatever she wrote, she decided not to send.

When I'm about to try a third time, she messages me. "WHAT."

Even from one texted word, she sound furious, and I almost turn my phone off for the rest of the day, for the rest of my life. But, no. I have to do this. So I take a deep breath and type, "I wanted to apologize."

Dancing ellipsis.

Dancing ellipsis.

"Oh," Rachel types. "Well, you have my attention."

And then I start typing. And I can't stop typing. "I'm sorry for being a jerk. And dumping your brother. And using you to dump your brother. And being a jerk. And...I can't think of anything else right now. But I'm sorry for all the stuff I can't think of. And I'm sorry for not being able to think of it right now. And I'm sorry for this gigantic wall of text I just made you read. I'm sorry."

Dancing ellipsis.

Then:

Rachel: Meghan.

Me: ?

Rachel: It's okay.

Just reading that, it's like someone lifted a sousaphone off my shoulders. A sousaphone and a sousaphone player.

Rachel: Your trombone teacher said something to Jonah. About your grandma. Why didn't you tell me?

Me: I couldn't talk about it.

Me: Not then.

Rachel: So tell me now.

Rachel: WAIT

Rachel: EVEN BETTER

Rachel: Tell me in 20 minutes when I pick you up.

And twenty minutes later we're breaking in Rachel's new driver's license on the way to Harpers Ferry, because, as Rachel says, "This is a reunion of epic proportions, and it needs to be celebrated. With ice cream, and creepy wax museums, and porcelain cows in Army uniforms." We start talking as soon as I get in her car, and I don't think we stop the whole way there. And we talk about everything.

Well. Almost everything...

Harpers Ferry is only half an hour away, but I haven't been there since the field trip we took in fifth grade. I remember it was hot, and I didn't have anyone to sit next to on the bus there, and in the last scene of the wax museum, when the John Brown figure jerked its head back and "The Battle Hymn of The Republic" started blaring out of nowhere, I got so freaked out I almost peed my pants.

So of course, right there in the wax museum, with creepy wax John Brown stepping up to the gallows, and an invisible chorus shrieking about the Second Coming, is where Rachel finally goes, "I know you didn't use me to get to Jonah. I know it's something that just...happened. And maybe you've moved on now, or whatever, but just so you know? He still totally likes you."

I struggle for something to say. Which is hard. Because it's suddenly about 400 degrees in here. "What about that other girl? The one with—" The one with the canned food? The one from the shopping center? The stupid one with her stupid three-inch heels stupid stupid stupid? "That Lizzi girl," I finally say.

Rachel squinches at me. "Lizzi Cohen? Please, she was ancient history by Tu B'Shevat. Which, by the way, I made an amazing film about."

"I'm sorry I missed it," I say, and I really am.

"But listen, they went out for two weeks, they had a fight at some dumb New Year's party, he spent a day listening to some sad Jonathan Coulton song on repeat, and then he started bugging me about you again. Like, were you in any of my classes this semester, were we talking again, blah blah blah."

It's about 500 degrees now. I thought this place had air-conditioning. "Well...what did you tell him?"

"I told him you and Brian hooked up in Baltimore over All-State weekend. At the aquarium. Against the shark tank."

"Okay, only like 50% of that is true," I say, before I can stop the words from tumbling out of my mouth.

"WHAT?" Rachel squawks. "Dude. I was kidding. I never told him any of that. I made that up right now. You and Brian...at All-State..." She collapses laughing against the wall. "Oh, God, please tell me the shark tank part was true."

"He has really, really good tone," I say. And then I give up and plop down on the floor next to her. Everything that's happened since Gram died—All-State, Brian, independent study, not getting into camp—seems so strange and far away now, like a bad movie I might have seen ten minutes of back in third grade. Man, I'm glad I messaged Rachel today. And I tell her so.

"I'm glad I messaged *you*," she says. "Now about my brother."

I don't think I'm ready to talk about Jonah yet. So I say, "Can we get out of here first? I think John Brown is staring at us." And once we're out of the museum, there's ice cream to eat at the general store, and cheesy souvenirs to buy, and then we talk about movies the whole way home.

#

I'm the first one at the band room Monday morning, and as soon as Mr. Coffman opens the door, I say, "This graduation band thing. Can I still do it?"

Mr. Coffman beams. "I knew you'd come around," he says. "First practice is tomorrow right after school."

I'm the first one in the band room after school on Tuesday, too. I know I decided to do graduation band because I wanted to Play With Other People Again, because it's All About Making Music Together, Man...but there's still no way I'm letting Jonah take first chair. So as soon as fourth period's over, I run to the band room and grab the first chair in the last row: the first trombone seat.

And I've just finished greasing and spraying my slide when some newbie kid I've never seen before walks up to me and says, "You can't sit there."

I want to ask him who the hell he is, and what the hell his problem is. Instead, I say, "What?"

"That's Jonah's seat. He's first chair." The kid stays rooted there, next to the chair, like he's going to intimidate me out of it. I stay where I am.

Then Jonah arrives.

"Adam, hey, what's up," he says, shrugging off his backpack and doing a stupid guy-handshake with the newbie kid. Then he looks at me. And it's the first time we've looked each other in the eye since November, and I'd probably fall out of the chair if I wasn't clinging to it. "You're doing graduation band?" He makes it sound like it's the worst news he's heard all year so far. Maybe it is.

"Yeah," I say. And then I have to look away. If we're having another staring contest, I think I've lost this time.

"Cool," Jonah says, though he clearly thinks it's anything but. And then he grabs a chair from the row in front of us, plunks it down on my left, and sits down.

I kind of want to kill him.

Satisfied, Adam sits down on my right, and then another newbie girl shows up and sits down on his right. She waves at Adam and Jonah, and doesn't even look at me.

Up on the podium, Mr. Coffman and Ms. Lozaro take turns talking about what an honor it is to be marching at graduation, and how it's going to make us an even stronger marching band come fall, and blah blah pride blah blah school spirit blah blah. Colleen introduces Kenzie as next year's head drum major, and A.J., and then a new junior drum major.

Dani.

I'm having some serious trouble concentrating. I can't look Jonah in the eye, but I can't stop looking everywhere else around him. He's got new glasses, ones that almost make it look cool to be nearsighted. His jeans are fraying, in that accidentally-on-purpose way I can never manage. It looks like he's started biting his nails again, and when he brings a thumbnail to his mouth, I almost reach out to pull it away and kiss it, like I used to.

Then I catch sight of his backpack, stuffed under his chair. Back in the fall, one afternoon at his house, I'd covered it with ballpoint doodles of that bear with the heart balloon, music notes, song lyrics we liked, dumb little hearts with our initials inside them. All of that's gone now —in the months since then, he's covered every single trace of me with Wite-Out.

What was that Rachel was saying, again? Something about him still liking me?

Yeah, I'm pretty sure she got that one wrong.

"So we're gonna head out to the field now," Mr. Coffman says, "and start working on some basic marching drills. You can leave your instruments here for now—we'll come back for some sight-reading later. All right, everyone?" He looks around the room, and when he spots us in the back row, he says, "Oh, good, trombones, you sorted it all out on your own."

Everyone turns around to see what he's talking about.

Jonah as first chair.

Me as second.

"YES, SIR!" Jonah yells, giving him a thumbs-up.

Well, fine, I think. Once we get on the field and start marching, we'll straighten this out, and everyone will know I'm in charge.

Then we get on the field. And I know I haven't even been out of band for a whole semester, but everything feels so off, I might as well be a newbie again. I'm totally out of shape, I can't keep up with the drills, my legs and arms won't listen to my brain, and people are yelling at me.

Specifically, Jonah.

Well, okay, it's not *really* yelling. But it's calling me out for doing something wrong. In front of everyone else. Kenzie runs through how to stand at attention—feet together, stomach in, chest out (no, thanks), elbows frozen, chin up, eyes with pride (whatever the hell that means), and Jonah becomes, like, obsessed with my elbows: "Elbows frozen, Meghan! Elbows frozen!" Then Dani goes through marking time, and Jonah's convinced I'm not doing it right. "Higher, Meghan!" Then, "Lower, Meghan!" Then, "Higher, Meghan!" again. Meanwhile, Adam can't tell the difference between attention and parade rest, and the other newbie, Maddie, can't tell the difference between her left and right feet. And Jonah isn't saying a thing about that.

So then—and I swear I'm not doing this to be petty—when we run through the music inside, I call Jonah out a few times. Four times, thank you very much. He may think he's some kind of marching god now, but I'm a better player than he is, especially when it comes to sight-reading. So: "Jonah, that's an F sharp, not an F natural." "Jonah, those are sixteenth notes, not eighth notes." "Jonah, you actually have to count the rests, remember?" And finally, "Ew, Jonah, seriously, F sharp!" And maybe Adam's playing everything in the wrong key, and maybe Maddie's too busy texting to play anything at all. But I don't care.

Yelling at Jonah only cheers me up a little bit, though. I'm still frustrated with myself, with Jonah, with Mr. Coffman, with this whole stupid situation, and it doesn't get any better as practices go on.

What really makes it hard is there's nobody there I can talk to about it. I mean, think about it. Who did I used to hang out with in band? Brian? I haven't even seen him since All-State. Ben and Jaden? They were Jonah's friends, not mine, and they're not doing graduation band, anyway. Jonah *is* the problem. And as for Dani...not that we ever really hung out in band, or at all after freshman year, but she's busy having her own power struggles with A.J. and Kenzie.

Charlie shows up at practice the week before graduation. The seniors are already finished with classes, but they still have to come into school for a few hours every morning for graduation rehearsal. DHS prides itself on its Traditional Graduation Ceremonies, which haven't changed since before the Civil War or whatever, and apparently the most important part of a Traditional Graduation Ceremony is making sure all the graduates process and recess very, very slowly. I'd think that would get old pretty fast, but I guess Charlie can't get enough of it, because he comes back to the field after school and spends two hours following Mr. Coffman up and down the sidelines, yelling out stupid stuff like, "Come on, let's hustle!" and "Make us proud, newbies!" Meanwhile, Mr. Coffman's yelling over him—"Newbies! What's going on? You should have this down by now!" And Ms. Lozaro's yelling over both of them—"Freshmen, you're doing great! Keep it up!" Kenzie and A.J. are arguing over which one of them gets to conduct "Pomp and Circumstance" from the podium. Jonah's reminding me that "horns parallel" means *parallel*, and then he says something about acute and obtuse angles that I don't catch, because I'm too busy reminding him for the hundredth time about that stupid F-sharp.

Mr. Coffman calls rehearsal early, out of what sounds like defeat. "Go home and get some rest, everybody," he says. "We'll try again tomorrow."

He doesn't ask us if we're the best marching band. He doesn't even say, "BAND! DISMISSED!" A few kids say "YES, SIR!" and "GO, PATRIOTS!" anyway. Mostly, we stampede out of the stadium.

Charlie falls in step beside me on my way back to school.

"Good work out there, Meghan," he tells me, like I asked for his opinion.

"Thanks," I say, like I believe it.

"So I'm starting at Towson in August. I'm gonna try out for their band."

"Cool."

Charlie says, "It's good to see you out in the world again. And not, like, hiding in the choir room doing lip slurs."

We've fallen in step with each other, without even meaning to. When you've spent a marching season keeping someone in your peripheral vision at all times, it's hard not to.

"The choir room's underrated," I admit. "For one thing, Jonah's never there." Maybe it's not the greatest idea to get into this with Charlie, but I have to talk about it with somebody who gets it, and he's my best bet.

"That whole section leader thing," he says, nodding wisely. "You want my advice?" He doesn't wait for an answer. "Don't worry about it. Graduation's in a week, and once band camp starts, if Brian sticks with jazz band, I bet you'll be section leader for real. I'll even talk to Matt about it for you, if you want."

It takes me a minute to remember that Matt is Mr. Coffman's first name. Oh, my God.

We stop outside Charlie's car, which he's parked right outside the band room. He strokes the scraggly excuse for a beard that's starting to grow along his chin and says, "You'll be fine next year. You're a trombone goddess."

A trombone goddess? Those words float around in my brain as I watch him drive away. Maybe that's what I wanted to be, once. But I'm not one. I'm just a girl who can play the right notes at the right time. And I can't even do that without Jonah yelling at me.

CHAPTER THREE

Graduation day is a half-day of school, and we spend the whole morning rehearsing. We're playing "Pomp and Circumstance" while the seniors march in, something called "Sine Nomine" while they march out, and "You'll Never Walk Alone" in the middle of the ceremony. "You'll Never Walk Alone" is the only one we're marching to, and with the seniors' seats taking up half the football field, we don't have room to do anything more complicated than a few pinwheels. But Mr. Coffman and the senior advisors keep us going for four hours.

Midway through the morning, the band finally gets to stand at ease while a senior girl I don't know runs through her graduation speech. It starts with, "As I look out on all of your bright, shining faces," and between that and the sun beating down on me, I last about ten seconds before I finally put down my trombone and sprawl out on the ground, right there on the football field.

"Uh, Meghan?" I open my eyes and squint in the sunlight. Jonah's towering above me.

"What?" I am so not in the mood for this.

"We're supposed to be at ease. Not asleep."

La la la, I can't hear him.

Maddie joins him. "Jonah's right," she says, though I

can't hear her, either. "Remember last week, Shane Wittkamper got yelled at for napping on his quads? And the whole section had to do 20 push-ups?"

Oh, for the love of God. I prop myself up on my elbows and say, as clearly as I can, "Who. The hell. Is going to make me do push-ups?"

And Jonah says, as clearly as *he* can, "I am."

Maddie looks up at Jonah with admiration, one step away from batting her eyelashes. "See?" she says to me. "Told you."

"Oh, shut up, newbie," I snap. It comes out louder than I mean it to. Loud enough that Dani's staring at me from the sidelines. Loud enough that even I can hear exactly what it sounds like—and exactly *who* I sound like.

Oh, crap.

Kenzie bellows, "BAND, ARE YOU READY, BAND!"

Even the idiots in my section know enough to stop what they're doing and respond. "YES, SIR!"

"Chart zero for 'You'll Never Walk Alone,'" she says. "That means everybody. You, too, Meghan."

I blush and try to stand up discreetly. Which, as it turns out, is hard to do when the whole band is looking at you. And when both your feet have fallen asleep. And when stupid Shane Wittkamper has left his stupid quad drums right behind you. So instead of standing up like a normal person, I take two wobbly steps behind me, catch my right foot on the drums, and fall flat on my face in the dirt.

From behind me, I can hear Adam and Maddie laughing.

I try to wipe my face on my t-shirt—the dirt, the sweat, my sunblock, and oh, God, a few tears, too—and while I'm trying to blink my way free of the mess in my eyes, Dani walks over, helps me up, and says, "Why don't you go back inside and clean up?"

I get to walk the entire length of the football field, so everyone in the band, and the whole senior class, can see what happened. I stare at my feet the whole way, so I don't have to see anybody's face, and when I get back inside to the girls' bathroom, I sink into a stall and cry.

When I get back to the field, they're in the middle of the song. I maneuver into place and start marching and playing along like a good little band nerd, even though inside I'm still a mess.

Kenzie cuts us off to go over a few measures with the flutes, and the other trombones go back to their usual idiocy. Jonah's grabbed Maddie's trombone, and he's making like he's going to toss it to Adam, while Maddie flails around between them, giggling helplessly. I think about what a section leader would do, and in as authoritative a voice as I can conjure up, I say, "Cut it out, Jonah. Give Maddie her trombone back and stop acting like a toddler."

That asshole Adam looks me straight in the eye and says, "Dude, why don't you go trip over some more quads?"

Maddie looks at Jonah, probably hoping he'll tell her how to react. For a second, I see the old Jonah in there— for a second, I think he's actually going to hug me or something. But then he shakes his head and turns away.

#

We get a one-hour break for lunch before the graduation ceremony. I'm not in the mood to talk to anyone, so while everyone else runs around getting rides to McDonald's or Starbucks or Jade Palace, I keep my eyes on my stupid feet, and take my brown-bag lunch, my headphones, and my French textbook out to the stairs by the parking lot. An ugly-ass old car zooms by—Shane Wittkamper's driving (and seriously, who the hell thought it would be a good idea to give him a driver's license, especially when he can't even keep track of his own stupid drums), and a bunch of other band kids are piled in the car, some sitting on each other's laps, all hanging out the window going, "Whooooooo!" I turn up a playlist Nina made for me and pretend to study for next week's exams.

I've been staring at the same photo on the same page of my French book for ten minutes by the time Dani comes out of the band room door, sunglasses on and her car keys in hand. She stops when she sees me, and mimes taking a pair of earbuds out of her ears. I do.

"Can I talk to you for a minute?" She doesn't wait for an answer, she just sits down next to me. "What are you listening to?"

I seriously doubt Dani's breaking months of silence to ask me what's on my headphones these days, but I answer her anyway. "Some of my sister's hippie music. It's actually kind of good." I hold out an earbud. "Wanna hear?"

"Um. No, thanks."

Of course not.

We sit together awkwardly for a few minutes. She studies her nails. I pretend I'm really interested in my French book. Finally, I give up and ask her. "What's up, Dani?"

She shifts in her seat. "It's not a big deal. But I'm supposed to talk to you about section stuff."

"Like what?" If I'd had any patience to begin with, it'd be wearing really, really thin now.

"Um. Well…you remember Kat?"

This can't be going anywhere good.

"Remember how she was always yelling at you and stuff?"

As if I could forget.

"And then Colleen put Charlie in charge instead?"

Oh, shit.

"Okay, look. Mr. Coffman was talking to the drum majors, and he said one thing he wanted to do with graduation band was figure out who the section leaders were gonna be for next year. And he wanted to know what we were thinking about you and Jonah. You know. After today."

I take a deep breath, and sit on my hands to stop them from shaking. "You're letting Jonah be section leader next year, aren't you."

"What? No!"

Oh, good, my heart is beating again. Neat. "But…"

"No but," she says, and suddenly we both giggle. "I have no butt." It's a dumb old joke of ours from middle school. I'd forgotten all about it.

"No, seriously," Dani continues. "Meghan, you're really good. You and Jonah. And I know it's probably weird, since you guys used to go out. I mean, I don't think I could ever be in the same section as Tyler or somebody."

In spite of myself, I wonder who Tyler is.

"I'm just saying…you and Jonah need to figure this out. Maybe you guys need to talk together, or maybe you need us to help—"

"I can do it," I interrupt her. "I'll talk to him today."

"Talk to him *and* listen to him," she clarifies. "I know you can do it, Meghan. You guys can figure this out."

And when she says that, I almost believe her.

Dani stands up. "Listen, I'm going to grab something at Jade Palace. Do you wanna come?"

I point to the brown bag crumpled at my side. "I finished lunch. But thanks."

"Lemme know how it goes with Jonah today." She hops down the steps and into her car, and waves to me as she drives away.

I'm left alone on the stairs, thinking uncomfortable thoughts.

Dani's just about exited the parking lot when Shane Wittkamper's car squeals back in. If possible, there's even more kids inside it than there were before. There's even a bunch of kids standing on top of the car. Shane swerves around the curve, and most of them manage to hang on while Shane makes a sharp right turn into Dani's old parking spot. But one of them—

Oh, God—

Jonah.

CHAPTER FOUR

I tear off my headphones and run for the car.

Shane's frozen in the driver's seat, clutching the steering wheel and chanting, "Oh, fuck, oh, fuck, oh, fuck." Adam looks like he's about to throw up. Maddie's slumped on the pavement, leaning against the car and hyperventilating.

I don't remember much about what happens next. People have to fill it all in for me later. Apparently, I order some newbie to call 911, and then I call the Rezniks' house, and when Rachel answers, I say, "Your idiot brother fell off a car. Meet us at Dulaney Memorial." Then I sit down on the ground next to Jonah—I remember the sun in my eyes —I remember holding his hand—I remember him making this terrible whimpering sound. But I don't remember telling Adam to get Maddie some water and calm her the hell down, or telling Charlie to get out of his stupid car and go find Mr. Coffman and tell him what happened.

The next thing I do remember is sitting with Rachel in the waiting room at the E.R., waiting for her parents to come back with news about Jonah, waiting for anything. The waiting room TV is tuned to PBS, that old show where the guy does paintings of happy little trees, and he's about to add a happy little rosebush when Mr. and Mrs. Reznik come in.

Mrs. Reznik squeezes Rachel, and then pulls me into the hug, too. "Thank you, Meghan," she says, and then she tells us the doctor says Jonah is going to pull through, he's got a mild concussion and he's going to need some stitches on his forehead, but he's going to be all right.

Mr. Reznik drives me home, and I try to explain to Mom and Dad what happened—it turns out Mr. Coffman had already called them and told them I was at the hospital. Then it hits me that I missed the graduation ceremony, and the band was missing the only two trombones who could actually march and play, and probably the whole band fell apart, and it was all Jonah's fault, all my fault, all our fault. Then I remember crying, in my mom's lap, on the couch, like a baby, and the next thing I know, it's five in the morning and I'm still lying on the couch, with Gram's old patchwork quilt wrapped around me and a full moon shining in the sky.

#

Jonah's at home recovering for the next few days. His parents say no visitors, but I send a card home with Rachel, and I sign it "Love, Meghan" without even thinking, and then I spend two days freaking out about that. I ask Rachel what he thought of the card, and she says, "He says thank you," and I have no idea what I'm supposed to do with that. Then she tells me, "He's coming in tomorrow, for the last day of school. Just so you know."

The last day of school is a joke, as it always is. It's like the teachers are even more ready than we are for the year to be done, so they just show movies and let us sign yearbooks.

At lunchtime, as rising juniors, Rachel, Ilana, Claire, and I get to try out our new off-campus lunch privileges for the first time. Everyone in our class has been hyped about this for months, but once Rachel's driven us over to Jade Palace, we realize that it'll take most of the lunch period just to drive somewhere and back, that we'll have to take our food to go and eat it in the car if we don't want to be later for class, and that egg rolls don't taste any more exciting during a school day than they do after school.

"Well, that was a letdown," Ilana says on our way back to school.

"Not to mention, some asshole probably stole my parking spot," Rachel grumbles.

We drive past the football field, and I think back to the beginning of band camp, and the beginning of the school year, when I was so sure things were going to change.

"Aren't things supposed to be, like, better now?" I ask everybody and nobody in particular. "I mean, we're gonna be juniors. Aren't we supposed to, like, have our shit together? And *know* things?"

"What do you mean?" Rachel asks. She giggles. "See, I don't even know *that*."

"I guess your answer's no," Ilana says.

"I don't know a damn thing," adds Claire.

We chew our food, and Rachel circles the school parking lot.

Then someone changes the subject, and pretty soon they're all talking about some movie I haven't seen. While they're talking, I keep thinking. Even if I don't have my shit entirely together, I must know *something* by now…right?

I know I love hanging out with my friends, even though they've got totally weird taste in movies.

I know my mom and dad are messed-up people, but there's nothing I can do to change them. And I know my sisters are pretty awesome people, and I wish I hadn't taken so long to figure that out.

I know that Gram's still watching me, even if she isn't doing it from a cloud in the sky.

And I know I need to talk to Jonah. For real. Today.

#

When the final bell rings, I head to the band room. My heart's pounding as I open the band room door. Stupid heart.

The plan is to wait until he shows up to pick up his trombone, and then maybe in the time before then, I'll be able to figure out what the hell I'm gonna say. But when I get inside the band locker room, he's already there. Still bandaged. Still adorable. Still Jonah.

We're the only people in the room, and our lockers are right next to each other, so there's no pretending or avoiding. "Hey, Jonah," I say. "What's up? I mean…how are you doing?"

He looks up from his backpack and trombone case. Behind his cool new glasses, his eyes look more tired than I've seen them before. He squinches, a little bit. God, I've missed that.

I try to read his expression—happy? nervous? nauseated? And while I'm wondering, I realize that, of course, I still don't know what else to say to him.

"Hey, Meghan," he says uncomfortably. He sighs, and sits down next to his stuff. And then he says it: "I'm sorry. About graduation band. And being an asshole."

I sit down next to him and find myself saying, "I've missed you. Like, a lot."

Wait. This is so not how it's supposed to happen.

He scoots away from me, a bit, but enough.

But I don't want that to happen, either. Do I?

And then he says, "You know, you broke my heart last fall."

Wait, what?

I did what?

"It was, like, months ago, and I'm still getting over you. Even when I was going out with Lizzi, I still liked you. That's why she dumped me. And even when I tried to be a jerk to you, I still liked you. I still *love* you. And I can't believe I just told you that."

Neither can I.

I open my mouth to say something—anything that'll

help me get control of this situation again. But I don't remember how to make words happen anymore. And then it doesn't matter anyway. Because I can't talk. Because Jonah's kissing me.

First I try not kissing him back. But that turns out to be impossible. So I kiss him back after all. It's a soft kiss that feels like home, and my Gram's old quilt, and everything that's quiet and right with the world, and oh, my God, I've missed this. I've missed being with Jonah, I've missed Jonah being Jonah, I've missed us being us...

But I need to face up to something, too. That's why I came here in the first place. So I pull away a bit and say, "I'm so sorry. If you were an asshole, I've been, like, the Asshole Queen."

His arm is still around my shoulders, and our noses are almost touching. I can tell the part of his brain that's still eight years old is trying to imagine what kind of crown an Asshole Queen would wear. And I know the rest of his brain, the warm and perceptive brain hiding underneath all the silliness, is trying to figure out what I mean, and waiting for me to finish. So I keep going.

"I mean—Homecoming—and then my Gram—and I never stopped liking you, either. I was scared. And stupid. And I didn't know what to do." I have to force all of these words up from my chest and out of my mouth, like I'm playing a series of high B-flats—high B-flat whole notes. And even though I feel like I'm splattering every single one, it still feels good to try.

"It's okay," Jonah says, pushing a misbehaving curl behind my ear like he used to. "I mean, like I said, it sucked. But I think I get it. I probably could've gotten it then, too, if you'd tried to explain it to me."

"Really?" I raise my eyebrows.

He thwaps me and says, "How come everybody thinks I have the emotional maturity of a cartoon character?"

"Probably because you're always talking about cartoon characters in serious conversations," I reply, grinning.

"Give me one example of a serious conversation," he says, "that couldn't be improved with a mention of a cartoon character."

He's smiling now. The first time he's smiled at me in months.

I take my thumb and trace his smile from ear to ear.

I don't know how long we sit there talking together. It feels like we're never going to run out of things to say. We talk about school and band gossip. I tell him about how much I loved playing the music at All-State, he tells me about SGA and the movie review vlog he's starting. He tells me how weird it feels to really be an upperclassman, I tell him how weird it was to get my first college viewbook in the mail last week. He asks about my Gram, and I tell him about being in Ocean City in November with a broken heart—and he does get it, as much as anyone can.

It isn't until the custodian peeks his head in the room that we realize how late it's gotten. "It's the last day of school," he says, in case we've forgotten. "You kids finish up and get home. Use the side door, out to the parking lot. It locks behind you automatically."

We shrug at each other, and then stand up and start gathering our stuff. Somehow I didn't notice until now, but he's grown about an inch since November, maybe more. I put my arms around his neck and smile at him like it's the most natural thing, like it hasn't been months since the last time. We stare at each other, nose to nose, giddy with possibility. And this time, I kiss him.

It's supposed to be a goodbye kiss, but then, like things always do with me and Jonah, the kiss takes on a life of its own. So we listen. And we pay attention. And we move together in time. Just like in marching band.

#

When I get home a few hours later, Rachel's sent me three texts.

1. "Dude, what is going on? Why is my brother smiling?"

2. "He's singing now. He won't stop. MAKE HIM STOP."

3. "OH MY GOD WHAT'S UP WITH MY BROTHER SERIOUSLY."

A ridiculous smile blooms across my face, and I text her back. "He's excited about marching band next year." And I am, too.

ACKNOWLEDGMENTS

This book would not exist without Chris Baty and National Novel Writing Month. It's gone through nine years of revisions since that flurry of a first draft, but without NaNoWriMo, it would never have made it out of my head and onto the page.

Megan Amoss, Lisa Jenn Bigelow, Kevin Farrell (the original top of the pyramid), Megg Jensen, Gordon Nash, Robyn Schoessow, Marie Selavy, and Jill Sinnott were all supportive and insightful early readers. Kristin Halbrook believed in Meghan and helped shape her story into something real. David Epstein, Tess Hoffman, and Peter McDade—the Potato Think Tank—brought this book back to life. Laura Seebol made sure everything was dotted and crossed correctly, and Sarah Marks created the fabulous cover.

Brian Riggins deserves special credit for letting me steal his name(s), and Joe Chellman deserves special blame for creating speed bowling.

Meghan's musical journey owes a lot to the teachers who shaped my own musical journey (particularly Kevin George, Chip Racster, and Brian Hinkley), and to all the fellow musicians I've worked with over the years.

My grandmothers, Florence Walsh Farrell and Anne Carey Healey, were rivaled in awesomeness only by Meghan's Gram. And my parents deserve extra-special thanks for years of shuttling me to and from auditions, rehearsals, and performances. How they kept their sanity raising three brass players in one house, I will never know.

Finally, all the love and gratitude to Neal Shankman, who supports and encourages me in everything I do.

ABOUT THE AUTHOR

Carey Anne Farrell writes, teaches, makes music, and co-hosts the podcast Go Your Own YA. Originally from Maryland, she now lives outside Chicago with her husband, their dog, and an ever-expanding collections of books, records, musical instruments, and creepy dolls. She is still recovering from her days in a bright yellow marching uniform.

Made in the USA
Lexington, KY
05 November 2018